Hazel

Also by David Huddle

My Immaculate Assassin (novel), 2016
Dream Sender (poems), 2015
The Faulkes Chronicle (novel), 2014
Black Snake at the Family Reunion (poems), 2012
Nothing Can Make Me Do This (novel), 2011
Glory River (poems), 2008
Grayscale (poems), 2004
La Tour Dreams of the Wolf Girl (novel), 2002
Not: A Trio (Two Stories and a Novella), 2000
The Story of a Million Years (novel), 1999
Summer Lake: New and Selected Poems, 1999
Tenorman (novella), 1995
A David Huddle Reader (stories, poems, and essays), 1994
Intimates (stories), 1993
The Nature of Yearning (poems), 1992
The Writing Habit (essays), 1992
The High Spirits: Stories of Men & Women, 1989
Stopping By Home (poems), 1988
Only the Little Bone (stories), 1986
Paper Boy (poems), 1979
A Dream With No Stump Roots In It (stories), 1975

David Huddle

Hazel

TUPELO PRESS
North Adams, Massachusetts
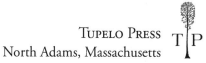

Cover and text designed by Ann Aspell.
Cover art: *Oeil de jeune femme* by Joseph Sacco, 1844. Tempera on ivory mounted on leather in leather and velvet case. Painting: 1¹/₄ × 1¹/₂ in. Case: 4³/₄ × 3¹/₂ × ³/₄ in. Used with permission of HIP / Art Resource, NY.

First edition: June 2019.

TUPELO PRESS
P.O. Box 1767
North Adams, Massachusetts 01247
(413) 664–9611 / Fax: (413) 664–9711
editor@tupelopress.org / www.tupelopress.org

Tupelo Press is an award-winning independent literary press that publishes fine fiction, nonfiction, and poetry in books that are a joy to hold as well as read. Tupelo Press is a registered 501(c)(3) non-profit organization, and we rely on public support to carry out our mission of publishing extraordinary work that may be outside the realm of the large commercial publishers. Financial donations are welcome and are tax deductible.

For Meighan Sharp, who created Hazel Hicks and was generous enough to allow me to contribute to her legend.

CONTENTS

Hazel

*Ms. Hicks considered herself
a vexed case.*

GOLDEN GLOVES

1957 — Burlington, Vermont

やっ

WHEN FELTON ASKED HER TO GO TO THE GOLDEN GLOVES, Hazel asked him to tell her more. She was fifteen. She'd never heard of Golden Gloves and didn't know what they were. When he explained, she was mildly interested and said yes. He'd asked her as if they were pals and did things like that together all the time. But of course they weren't and they didn't.

Hazel wouldn't have allowed herself to think so at the time, but she could hardly bear most of the people around her. Or for that matter most aspects of her life. She thought the misery she felt all the time was her fault. Felton's invitation was the first evidence she'd had that somebody her age might want to do something with her.

Felton walked to her house. When she heard his heavy steps on the porch, she came out to meet him. Hazel knew her mother was watching from the side window. Which made her happy. It was starting. She was going to have her own life. Nothing her mother could do about it. While they walked, Felton told her about the fighters they would see.

He was the only person she knew who paid any attention to the Golden Gloves. Kids at school were ignorant like she was. Her father had nodded when she told him where she was going. He probably knew it was boxing matches. Her Uncle Freddy might have known. He was a veteran and a hard drinker who hung around with other hard drinkers in town.

Maybe her Uncle Freddy would be there, they'd see each other, and it would be embarrassing. No big deal. She was out of the house and walking downtown in the twilight with a boy who was taller than her father and who probably weighed twice as much as she did. The air smelled like popcorn. Felton was telling her about *The Star Spangled Banner* and the girl who would sing it.

The Lefebvre family ran the Golden Gloves here in town. They fascinated Felton; she could tell by his excitement as he told her about them. They rented Memorial Auditorium, they assigned which fighters fought which, they hired the referees, a Lefebvre wife sold tickets, Lefebvre children and grandchildren handed out programs at the doors.

Lefebvres owned the boxing ring, and Lefebvres set it up for the matches. And of course Lefebvres selected the person who got to sing the national anthem, though rumor was that the Lefebvres had squabbled over the choice. For the last ten years Tressie Lefebvre had sung it, but there was a young cousin who was thought to be a better singer.

Hazel can hardly believe that she has remembered so much about the Lefebvre family. She'd thought she wasn't really listening to Felton as he went on and on with his explaining. She's pretty sure she was bored in the same way she usually was in school. Jack Lefebvre had taken over the matches from his grandfather Henry, but who cared?

Felton Wadhams cared and as he talked, Hazel figured out that he'd stored up all this information but never had anyone to tell it to. While the Lefebvre legend was spilling out of him, she wondered if she was just his victim or if maybe he had enough of a crush on her to want to tell her about something that was important to him.

When they turned onto South Union Street, they saw crowds of people pressing toward the auditorium doors. It shocked Hazel to see so much commotion and energy generated by an event she knew nothing about. And they were only six blocks from her house. "This way," Felton said, stepping ahead and leading her past the crowd and around to a side door.

She could have sworn he wanted to take her hand to help her follow him. She thought she felt his fingers brush the back of her hand. She understood he wanted her to witness this special treatment the Lefebvres gave him. He was proud of himself. She thought that was all right. If he had touched her hand, she'd have probably let him take it.

At the side door Felton showed his tickets to a man with a cigarette in his mouth. The man nodded and Felton led her upstairs. Up on the main floor it was crowded and loud, a little bit crazy. She was glad for Felton's bulk. She got behind him and kept close. It amused her that she didn't mind following him. He kept glancing back to check on her.

At the door into the gym a kid she recognized from school handed her a program. Chip Lefebvre—that was his name. A junior. He hardly looked at her. He had no idea she knew about his family controlling the Golden Gloves. Her family didn't control anything. Felton Wadhams made her feel safer in this crowd than her mother or father would have.

They were six rows up from the boxing ring. Felton told her he didn't want to sit any closer because sometimes when a punch landed, blood flew out of fighter's face and splashed on people who sat ringside. "I don't mind sweat," Felton told her, "but somebody's blood on my shirt freaks me out." He grinned at her when he said these things.

Where they sat she could see maybe a thousand people. Hazel was excited. This was fine with her. If she hadn't followed Felton Wadhams into that crowd of riled-up boxing fans, she might have spent her whole life never feeling this way. Like she was part of something huge she couldn't control. Whatever happened next she was eager to see it.

She knew she had a grin on her face, and her eyes couldn't get enough of watching all those people milling in the aisles and around the boxing ring. Tough old ladies with shriveled-up husbands, men wearing jackets and ties, guys with tattoos who wore wife-beaters, tattooed young women with hair-dos and outfits like she'd never seen before.

When every seat was taken the noise was so loud that Felton stopped trying to talk to her, but he leaned a little bit toward her. Hazel surprised herself by leaning slightly his way. When their elbows touched, she was startled but she didn't move away from him. Shouting kids ran up the staircases and through the aisles like they had no parents.

When the announcer introduced the singer for the national anthem, it wasn't Tressie Lefebvre—it was Gina Lefebvre. Felton gave Hazel a look of mock astonishment that made her laugh out loud. Gina Lefebvre appeared to be maybe fourteen, very slender with long, straight black hair, a pale face, and a touch of lipstick. She looked scared.

Hazel saw Gina's hand tremble when she took the microphone from the announcer. This girl was going to butcher the national anthem. Hazel felt embarrassed for her. She thought the cruelty of changing singers would be worse for Gina than it was for Tressie. When Gina finally lifted the microphone to her face, the crowd went still.

People around her stood up dutifully. Felton and Hazel also stood. She felt herself cringing when the first notes of Gina's quavery, childish voice wafted through the auditorium. She couldn't imagine how she or anyone else could endure the minutes it would take for the child to finish the song. A huge, soft groan arose from the crowd.

The announcer leaned toward Gina and whispered. Gina stopped singing and raised the microphone closer. She'd gotten only as far as "can you see." Now she started over. Hazel wanted to scream. When she glanced at Felton she saw he'd closed his eyes.

Then she saw that Gina had closed her eyes, too—as if Felton had sent her a sign.

At "dawn's early light," the voice filling the building suddenly became that of a grown woman. The girl's rich, gliding alto made Hazel shiver. She saw that Gina's eyes weren't merely closed, she was squinching them shut so tightly her whole face was contorted. As if she were facing a firing squad that was about to execute her.

No singer herself, Hazel sensed that her mouth was shaping the words of the national anthem as Gina sang them. When she glanced up at Felton, she saw that his mouth was also moving— and that a tear was leaking out of his eye. A big guy like him! She felt queasy at the thought of weeping at Gina's song. She willed herself not to do so.

All around them people began shouting and clapping while Gina triumphantly sounded, "and the home..." The noise became so thunderous that Hazel never heard the final words of the song. She was filled with a peculiar emotion she thought must be patriotism. Gina lowered the mic, opened her eyes, and smiled as if she'd just won a contest.

Along with the crowd Hazel and Felton settled back into their seats. People fluttered their programs, chattered, and laughed in a way that made her think of a flock of gulls landing at North Beach on the lake. "There you have it," said Felton as if he were responsible for Gina's grand success. Hazel didn't mind. He'd brought her here.

The announcer's amplified voice overrode all the noise in the building, but Hazel could make out only some of what he said. First it was stupid thank-yous with a lot of names, then it was introductions of the judges and the referee. Felton wasn't interested either. He was using the program to show her which matches were most important.

Having had no previous experience of being somewhere with a boy or a young man, whichever Felton was, Hazel became aware that her attention was wandering. But she was acutely aware of the intensity of his voice and the proximity of their bodies, and she liked the way he pronounced the name of his favorite fighter, Ace Lucas.

She couldn't focus on the actual information he was trying to convey to her. She laughed aloud when he demonstrated the difference between a jab and a hook, punching his fist forward for the jab and swinging it sideways and around for the hook. He kept coming back to the topic of Ace Lucas. "He can take a punch," he told Hazel in a low raspy voice.

That was the moment she felt shocked by her intimacy with Felton. His face was so close to hers she could smell his breath! She was suddenly aware of how profoundly different his body was from hers and how he really could hurt somebody with his fists. Her face went hot, and she was so uncomfortable she almost stood up and left the building.

That was when Felton caught her eye and gave her that half-smile of his. She was pretty sure she understood him. There was no threat in his face. His half-smile meant he wanted her to be his pal. He wasn't asking for love or sex. She felt sure he was every bit as innocent and lonely as she was. Neither of them had anybody to talk to.

She sat in her woozy reverie, now and then murmuring or just making a humming noise in her chest in response to Felton's chatter. Who knew he had so much to say? He seemed to be trying to tell her everything that had passed through his brain. He was talking about throwing the shot put for the track team when the first boxing match began.

These were teenage boys with their shorts pulled up almost to their chests. A redhead and a boy with black hair that kept falling over his eyes. They waved their huge boxing gloves in front of each other's faces as if they really meant no harm. They stepped toward and away from each other, bending their upper bodies this way and that.

Hazel felt sorry for them—they looked so scared and child-ish. They could have been Gina Lefebvre's classmates. They weren't trying very hard to hit each other with their gloves, but they both seemed intent on avoiding their opponent's blows. Voices rose from the crowd. A woman shouted, "Hit him, Carl! Knock the stuffing out of him!"

The bell rang. The fighters turned away from each other and quickly took their seats on stools their handlers set into opposite corners of the ring. They leaned back against the ring posts and let their arms dangle as if they were exhausted. So far as Hazel could tell, neither of them had landed a blow on the other. Felton was grinning.

A stocky woman from the front row stood and walked be-hind the corner of the black-haired boy. His handlers stood aside while she spoke to him. Hazel couldn't hear her, but from the way her head moved, she knew the woman was egging him on. "It can only be his mother," Felton said. "So that's Carl?" Hazel asked, and Felton nodded.

When the bell rang the redhead stepped forward as he had in the first round, but Carl ran toward him in a crouch and threw a roundhouse blow that struck the boy in the ribs, made him groan, and drop his hands. Then Carl punched him in the face, straight on and very hard. The redhead fell backward and lay on his side, unmoving. His nose bled.

The violence of what Hazel had seen seemed to have oc-curred within her own body, slightly above her solar plexus. She had to struggle to bring air into her chest. In a panic she looked at Felton, whose face was flushed. He was leaning forward, con-centrating on the ring, as if he meant to go down there to see if the boy was all right.

The crowd bellowed and writhed, but when the handlers summoned a doctor to the side of the fallen boy, most people stopped shouting and clapping and sat down. A man swabbed blood off the redhead's face. When the doctor waved something under his nose, the boy moved his arms and legs. People applauded. The handlers helped him up.

While Carl pranced around the ring with his hands over his head, the announcer proclaimed his victory, and the redhead's assistants helped him down out of the ring. Hazel stood quietly beside Felton. She was aware of noise, movement, and even the wild mix of smells in the air. Down in the ring Carl's mother stood, her face shiny with tears.

Hazel thought herself a fool for not having anticipated that she'd see fighters trying to harm each other. She wondered if Felton should have warned her, because certainly he knew what happened down in that ring. What he couldn't know was how little experience she had. Until now she hadn't realized how much her parents had protected her.

She figured she'd never forget Carl's rushing toward that red-haired kid, knocking him down, then the gush of blood from the boy's face. Those moments kept playing in her mind even after Felton signaled to her that it was time for them to sit down. But she wasn't horrified. If something like that happened again, she thought she was ready for it.

Fresh fighters arrived in the ring. They bounced on their feet and punched the air in front them. Unlike Carl and the redhead, these two wore short shiny bathrobes. One was tall and skinny, the other a solid-looking fellow whose face Hazel vaguely remembered from the hallways at school. She wondered if their mothers were in the crowd.

She became aware of Felton studying her face. She turned to him. He wasn't smiling, but his face was open to her. Actually, she realized, she'd never really taken a good look at him before. His eyes were a little too close together, but his cheeks were rosy. "Are you all right?" he asked. She grinned at him. "I have no idea," she said.

Felton knew not to ask more questions, and he seemed to have passed through his phase of extreme chattiness. He did, however, sit closer to her than he had before. Their shoulders touched occasionally during the matches that followed. If that hadn't been the case, she might have asked him to walk her home. The touching made her want to stay.

Hazel watched the fighting only when the crowd became excited. Mostly she let her eyes sweep the auditorium looking for the highly animated people who sat in every section. She wished Carl's mother would return so that she could study her more carefully. Felton gave his attention to the fights, which licensed her to do as she pleased.

Then Felton nudged her and nodded toward the entrance for the fighters at the far end of the auditorium. Over there, some people were moiling around and chanting. Felton said, "He's in the building!" It took her a moment to understand he meant Ace Lucas. The chant she'd been hearing was "Ace! Ace! Ace!" Felton's face was that of a happy child.

She almost laughed at him, but she didn't. He'd been waiting for Ace all this while—Ace was the whole point of this evening, including her part in it. She was suddenly able to relax. Felton's tension had affected her, and now they were both free. Free to do what, she didn't know, but Hazel shocked herself by applauding like a cheerleader.

She excused herself to go to the ladies room, which was a little like venturing into a dangerous neighborhood and finding her way out again. Strange people stared at her and not in a friendly way. She worried that she wouldn't be able to find her way back, but she did. And when she sat down beside Felton, she relished how safe she felt.

Back in her seat Hazel let her mind journey to her room at home, not merely the bed, which she now recognized as a source of deep comfort to her, but also her dresser-top with its knickknacks arranged just so, her clothes in her closet, the little rug beside the bed that spared her feet from the cold floor, the chair where her pajamas waited for her.

Jolted from her reverie by a swell of noise and everyone around her suddenly standing up, she saw Felton looking down at her with a quizzical expression. The crowd thundered, "ACE! ACE! ACE!" When Hazel stood and rose on tiptoe to catch a glimpse of the ring, there stood Ace in crimson trunks, his face shining up toward the lights.

Her first thought was that he looked a little silly. He was skipping around the ring, his taped hands raised over his head as if he'd already won the fight. He wasn't the strapping young fellow she'd expected. His skin was pale, his legs were thin, and though his shoulders and arms were heavily muscled, he was sunken-chested and he had a belly.

Ace's eyes were slitted and his face was a flesh-colored mask. She thought he was at least thirty-five, maybe even forty years old. When the crowd stopped shouting his name, he dropped his hands and went to stand with his corner men. That was when Hazel realized he'd been keeping his belly sucked in as he pranced around with his arms raised.

She glanced up at Felton, who grinned at her, shook his head, and shouted above the noise, "I know, I know!" She appreciated his having discerned her disappointment, but she also took him to mean that she would soon see the truth of Ace Lucas. Throughout the evening Felton had risen in her opinion. She didn't think he'd be wrong about Ace.

When the bell rang, Ace swaggered out to meet his opponent, a stocky young fellow representing a boxing club in Newburgh, New York. The referee signaled the fighters to touch gloves at the center of the ring. Then the ref stepped back, and so did the opponent, but Ace instantly lunged forward with a punch aimed at his opponent's head.

The crowd roared, Felton along with them. Evidently they'd been expecting Ace's signature move. Hazel had been shocked by the obvious dirtiness of the punch, whereas all around her people were laughing gleefully. The opponent had mostly dodged the blow, though it had scraped his cheek and his ear. He seemed bemused by Ace's foul play.

Felton leaned down toward her and said, "Sometimes that's all he has to do to win the fight." Hazel tried to smile, but all she could manage was a nod. In the ring, Ace doggedly stepped forward, always leading with his right foot and feinting with his gloves and body. Now and then he lunged toward the other fighter with a powerful punch.

The opponent, however, was light on his feet and easily dodged Ace's crude punches, meanwhile landing dart-like blows all over Ace's face. The opponent's strategy was to avoid whatever Ace threw at him, meanwhile punishing Ace with his sharp jabs. Even Hazel could see that the opponent was learning Ace's methods and that he'd soon make a move.

Hazel became aware of Felton moving his body. At first she thought something must be wrong with him—these were whole-body gyrations he was making, as if he might be in gastric distress or something worse, like a kidney stone or a collapsed lung. But when she glanced at his face she saw that he was completely focused on the two men in the ring.

The bell rang to end the round. Ace stood still for a beat until his opponent dropped his gloves and turned toward his corner. The punch Ace threw had his whole weight behind it. Had it struck the target Ace had in mind, it would have dropped the fellow to the mat, but his reflexes saved him. He raised an arm to deflect the blow from his chin.

The referee immediately stepped in front of Ace and pushed him back toward his corner—then stood right in front of him shaking his finger in Ace's face and shouting at him. Ace sat on his stool and stared back at the referee. He looked like a pouting fourth-grader. The handlers spoke to the referee, pleading with him not to stop the fight.

Hazel entered a state of consciousness she'd never experienced. One track of her thinking was that Ace was an utterly unscrupulous fighter—and that Felton and most of the people around her admired him for that. And though she wasn't ready to admire Ace, she did finally understand his appeal. Like the Lefebvres, he was a local phenomenon.

They were of this town in a way that she and Felton and their parents and their friends would never be. Not quite criminals or outlaws, their families had lived right here while riding forward on some current of time that went back at least a century. They were throwbacks who came from bootleggers, squatters, poachers, petty swindlers.

Hazel kept trying one word and another, but nothing was quite right for a person like Ace Lucas. The other track of her thinking had to do with Felton and the twisting and bending of his torso, all the while holding his arms tightly folded in front of him as if he was trying to keep himself in check. And he never stopped watching the fight.

But all his gyrating had ceased the instant the ref stepped in front of Ace and pushed him back to his corner. Felton kept his eyes on the ring, but his body stopped moving. And now that the bell had rung again and the fighters had started circling each other, dodging, feinting, jabbing, and punching, Felton had again begun to writhe in his seat.

She knew he'd be embarrassed if he noticed her watching him, so she did it surreptitiously. But he was so intent on the fight that he might not have noticed if she'd stood up and yelled, "Stop that!" The idea made her snort quietly. That's when she realized Felton's body here beside her was invisibly linked to Ace's body down in the ring.

So it was a weird and involuntary empathy working on him. The trance he was in was so powerful that he probably wasn't even aware of what his body was doing. Hazel was fifteen years old. What was she supposed to make of this squirming boy? Was this a young man thing? Was it a boxing thing? She shook her head in a kind of wonderment.

The swelling of the crowd noise made Hazel look back to the fight. The spectacle down there made no sense, but she couldn't look away. Ace had dropped his gloved hands to his sides, and he stood in one place, slightly bouncing from one foot to the other. His opponent struck him again and again, landing jabs on Ace's face, chest, and belly.

Ace was bleeding—the word that came to Hazel was *magnificently.* Bright lights shone on the red streams from his nose, his mouth, the cuts on his face. She realized the opponent wasn't hitting Ace all that hard. Ace seemed to be taunting the man, trying to egg him on. Finally the opponent stopped jabbing. He stood and stared at the ref.

As if he'd just regained consciousness, the ref raised his hands to call the fight over and directed the boxers back to their corners. The crowd booed mightily, though Hazel was relieved to see that Felton kept his mouth shut. He continued staring down toward the ring. So she faced him and wondered how long it would take him to notice her.

She hoped he could explain to her what she'd just witnessed. She shivered with the thought that maybe it had been a kind of religious experience. She'd always hated the crucifixion story, because of its crazy violence. She couldn't place herself anywhere in it, not as Jesus or a soldier or somebody in the crowd or God or Pontius Pilate.

But she'd seen Ace Lucas punished and bleeding, and though the sight of it had pained her, she'd nevertheless kept watching until the ref put a stop to it. Finally Felton looked down at her. His face was bathed in sweat, and he seemed startled to find her there beside him. She met his eyes and made her expression as neutral as she could.

She could see Felton trying to come back to himself and to understand who she was and why she would be standing here staring at him. He had the dazed expression of an astronaut newly returned from outer space. He blinked and tried putting on a grin, but his mouth seemed to have lost the skill. Then she saw it coming back to him, who she was.

"Are you all right?" he asked. His voice was raspy and much louder than it needed to be. Irked though she was because he'd so completely put her out of his consciousness, she couldn't help feeling a little sorry for him. "I was starting to ask you the same question," she said. "So do you think this will be Ace's last fight?"

Felton glanced down at the ring, then back at Hazel. Now she saw that he'd gotten his wits back. "Wasn't that something, though?" His voice bespoke pride and affection. The boy might have been speaking of an older brother who'd accomplished something amazing. Just then a cluster of loud-talking people started up the aisle beside them.

When she saw Felton's eyes look over her head, Hazel turned to see what was going on. This group of very excited people included both men and women moving up the steps. At the center was someone with a towel over his head. It took her a moment to understand this was Ace Lucas leaving the ring, and these noisy citizens were his entourage.

"Why's he going out this way?" she asked. "Don't the fighters go out over there?" she pointed to the door where the boxers entered and exited. "And why are all his people acting like he won the fight?" Now she was the disoriented one. She felt like she'd entered the *Star Wars* bar where all the customers were monsters who spoke English.

Felton couldn't keep from watching the dozen or so people accompanying their fighter up the steps that led out to the lobby. Ace's face wasn't visible to Hazel, but she thought maybe Felton had gotten a glimpse of it. A part of her wanted to see the cuts and bruises inflicted on him, but the thought shamed her. Felton finally turned to her.

"I think they're going to parade him through the lobby," he told her. "I don't know why." His voice was soft, and his expression was puzzled, but she was exasperated with him. He'd brought her here, and now he wasn't helping her. "Why did he just stand there and let that guy beat him up?!" In her voice she heard a shrillness she could hardly bear.

Felton sat down in spite of everybody in the whole building moving toward the exits. "He's done that before." He stared up at Hazel with a stunned face. "Nobody really knows why he does it. Maybe just to show that nobody can knock him out." Felton shook his head. "It just seems to come over him. And you saw how everybody goes crazy."

Felton suddenly stopped meeting her eyes and turned his face away. "He wins fights when he wants to." His voice was petulant now. As if she shouldn't be asking him these questions. Then he said something else too softly for her to hear, so she cocked her head. He shouted out into the nearly empty auditorium, "Ace does what he decides to do!"

While she stared down at him, Felton bowed his head. This view let her consider what must have been his anger over having to explain Ace Lucas to her. Maybe he'd never tried to put it into words before. Now he fidgeted, put his arms around himself, jittered his knees. Was he about to start squirming in his seat again? She looked away from him.

Gradually she sensed him wanting her to sit beside him again. The auditorium was nearly empty. If she just waited, Felton would stand up, and he'd probably walk her home. If not, she knew the way. In her mind she was already putting on her pajamas, shivering in that way she sometimes did just before she got under the covers.

John Robert's Project

My Aunt Hazel Hicks claimed that she did not collect photographs of any kind and certainly not photographs of herself. Initially I believed her. She was a proud and, as my parents liked to say, voraciously articulate, person, who worked for the Vermont Department of Education in the Office of Legislative Reports for more than half a century. She was entirely without vanity. Whenever she encountered a photograph of herself, her response was to laugh. I know this because in her later years, when I became aware of what an unusual life she had led, I began assembling documents that would testify to her achievements and her singularity.

My project amused her—she told me that she'd accomplished nothing she would consider an achievement and the only way she was singular was in the number of people who couldn't stand her. As it turned out, I did find several letters of complaint in her file in Montpelier, a couple of which I showed her. The letters interested her so much that she wanted to discuss them with me. She had clear memories of the people who had written them, and (true to her personality as I had come to know it) she spoke of them with grim respect.

"It's the ones who didn't have the nerve to put their words on paper but who liked to run their mouths in public meetings— they're the ones I'd have fired if I'd had my way." But it was the photographs of her that always brought forth her laughter. She'd say, "Would you hire this person to clean your septic tank?" and "What in the world does she think she's doing?" and "Would you look at that face?" I once told her that the way she responded to those pictures made me think that if she saw a movie of her life, she'd say it was a comedy. That made her guffaw.

"People would pay money not to see that movie, John Robert. But what else do you think it might have been? What do you think the movie of your life would be?" And that was the kind of person my Aunt Hazel was. She could turn your own words back on you in such a way that you'd lose sleep thinking about who you thought you were as opposed to who you really were. In my opinion, with Aunt Hazel, there wasn't any difference or slippage. She was exactly who she thought she was. Few people ever got to know her, and fewer still understood her, which was, she told me, exactly how she wanted it. "I had a great deal of freedom," she told me.

Young Hazel

This black and white one is in the hospital hours after she was born. She's swaddled up tightly in that generic thin cotton hospital baby blanket bordered with lines that are probably pink and blue. For the photographer, her father (my granddad) holds her high enough that her face is at the same level with his face. Aunt Hazel has a bit of dark hair, and her face and head are dark as if she's flushed from crying. But my father (her younger brother) assures me that even as an infant she didn't cry much. In this photograph her expression is comically hostile, and her eyes are fixed on her father, as if they are already seriously at odds with each other.

My father tells me that the picture did not accurately prophesy the future relationship between father and daughter. "They got along pretty well," he says, "and the same was the case with your Aunt Hazel and our mother. Hazel left it to us boys to do all the arguing and rule-breaking and disgracing the family with our behavior. Your Uncle Walt and I knew she had the same conflicts with our parents that we did, and their rules for her were even stricter than they were for us. Not that they were parental dictators, but they kept an eye on us and expected us to live up to a certain standard.

"Hazel argued with them about the fact that her curfew times were hours earlier than Walt's and mine were—those conversations were more like debates compared to the one that Walt and I had with them about our curfews. Hazel figured out very quickly that she was not going to persuade them to change their minds or change the rules. So she just went upstairs to her room and closed the door. No stomping, no slamming the door, no turning up the music once she got in there. Your Aunt Hazel was a navigator, not a drama queen. She didn't like getting mad. She was quick to speak her mind if she disagreed with you, and she'd discuss the issue with you, but she wouldn't argue.

"If she thought you were an idiot, she'd just stay away from you. Neither Walt nor I ever knew what she did in that room once she went in and closed the door. Read books or wrote in her diary was what we supposed she did. But we weren't sure she even had a diary. A few times, when we knew she wouldn't catch us, we tried finding her diary. But either she didn't have one at all or she hid it so well we couldn't find it. She probably did have secrets, but she kept them secret. You'd never call her a Miss-Goody-Two-Shoes or even a good girl, but she was a genius at staying out of trouble. She left the job of getting into trouble to your Uncle Walt and me."

CONCERTO

1959 — Burlington, Vermont

ℭℑ

I could probably tell my wife, but so far I haven't. It's a big deal to me, but I'll bet if I ever do tell her she'll be only slightly interested, and it won't stick with her. She'll say something like, "So, Carter—this was back in high school, right?" Meaning it's over, it happened a long time ago, we don't have to talk about it.

Okay, on several occasions Hazel Hicks and I went into a room by ourselves and stayed more than an hour. We spoke only when necessary. We had no physical contact. Our band director and maybe one or two kids knew where we were, but for us it was like we had strapped ourselves into a capsule that was orbiting around the planet.

For our senior recital, Mr. White assigned Hazel and me Vivaldi's *Concerto for Two Trumpets*. When he handed us the sheet music he winked at us. "With this piece you kids gonna blow them away," he said. Hazel and I glanced at each other. Not something we did very often. We knew that piece was going to be tough.

When I think back, I realize she and I were like puppets, with Mr. White and Vivaldi and the school and our parents pulling the strings. If you'd asked us what we'd like to do, neither of us would have even thought of playing a duet. Not that we were against it. It was just an alien concept to us.

Mr. White couldn't really know how little Hazel and I had to do with each other in our regular lives. Our worlds were separate in every way except that we were both in the band. And even in band she and I never talked. Okay, I was a popular kid, and Hazel was a loner. I didn't mind attention; she tried to be invisible.

So as a human being, Hazel hardly existed in my thinking, but I did know about her as a musician. There were more than a hundred kids in our band, maybe a dozen of whom were serious about music. We knew who we were. She and I didn't have to be friends to be aware of each other's level of ability.

I was First Chair, First Trumpet; she was First Chair, Second Trumpet. No question I was the stronger musician, but she was no slouch of a trumpet player. She had talent, but she never showed us what she could do. She was smart, technically skilled, and dependable, but she always seemed to be holding back.

Mr. White had raised money for our school to convert some old storage space into a couple of practice rooms. They were nothing fancy—they each had a piano, some music stands, and a few chairs. The walls had these gray echo-absorbing panels. When you flipped on the light switch and stepped in there it felt like a prison cell.

Our first practice session Hazel stood aside and let me go in ahead of her. I took that the way I did a lot of things back in those days—that she was acknowledging my being a rock star of the band and the school. Recently it occurred to me that it was probably because the room creeped her out. She let me be the canary in a coal mine.

I confess I'd never taken a careful look at Hazel. It wasn't because I knew staring at her would be rude. And it wasn't because she was ugly or unsightly. I'd probably glanced at her a few times and seen nothing to hold my attention. Nowadays I think maybe she willed her face and her body to send no signals of any kind.

She dressed somewhat plainly, wore no makeup, spoke softly when she spoke at all. She had a friendly smile that appeared infrequently and always disappeared in a flash. I think she was a watcher who had all of us figured out—especially those of us in the band—but she gave no sign of what she thought of us.

I also think she was a genius at navigating through the unpredictable and dangerous corridors of high school life. Kids were always getting bullied or insulted or excluded or ostracized or gossiped about; there were cliques, there were teachers who were mean or bitter or moody. Hazel sailed through it all with hardly anyone noticing her.

So the two of us in the practice room by ourselves was something new for both of us, and we came to it from opposite directions. I was Mr. Social; she was Miss Loner. But there we were, with such a bright fluorescent light above us that it made me think of an operating room—a thought I kept to myself.

Maybe because of that light we kept quiet while we set up the chairs and stands. We didn't have to discuss how we wanted to sit—side by side, facing the music. We both understood what ought to transpire in our hour of practice, but we had to work out the details by ourselves. A normal situation, of course, and probably very educational.

So much of our band activity in particular and our school life in general was dictated by teachers and administrators and what people call the herd mentality. You do what you're told to do or you do what everybody else is doing. You get with the program. But a boy and a girl in room with a closed door is something else entirely.

I became aware of my heart beating, and I had no idea why. Nerves, I guess, but there was nothing in the arrangement that should have made me nervous. I was vice-president of the junior class, a straight-A student, and I'd heard Mr. White say I was a hell of a trumpet player. When I glanced at Hazel, I was pretty sure her heartbeat was normal.

Standing in opposite corners of the room we took out our instruments and warmed up for a couple of minutes. Made a tuneless racket. Then we sat down, opened up the sheet music, stared at it a minute or so. Pretty much in unison we raised our horns. "All set?" I asked. I waited a moment, then I murmured the count, and we were into it.

The piece begins with three descending quarter notes played in unison, but very quickly there are these alternating bars of sixteenth notes and triplets, and both players have to be very solid in their upper registers. But technically, it's not all that challenging, and so Hazel and I played through the first section without stopping.

"Hunh," I said while we were both lowering our horns. I thought we'd played together pretty darned well for our first run-through. It seemed to me we probably wouldn't need more than just one or two more practice sessions before we could perform it. I had better things to do than spend an hour in a practice room with Hazel Hicks.

When I grinned at Hazel, she winced, and shook her head ever so slightly. Then she tapped the music on my stand at bar 18. We'd never discussed which of us was to play the lead part because there was nothing to discuss—it was mine. So I was shocked when Hazel lifted her trumpet and played my part for bars 18 through 22.

I understood immediately—she was correcting me! I hadn't realized how sloppy I'd played those runs of eighth notes and sixteenth notes. Hazel's quick execution of my part made it clear that I had some work to do. I couldn't be angry, because she was obviously right. She tapped the music in the same place and raised her horn.

Okay, I understood what she had in mind. I raised my horn, too, and tapped my foot for the count. We played through those four bars again. I executed the quarters and the sixteenths better than I had the first time, but I had to face the news that I needed more practice. We sat in silence for what seemed a good two minutes.

We held our trumpets bell down on our thighs, and our postures were perfectly straight, the way Mr. White had trained us to sit for performances. "Professional" was a word he enunciated for us in a way that conveyed how desirable it was. So Hazel and I, two seventeen-year-olds, were having a few moments of "professional" silence.

I wasn't a kid who sat still very often, and when I did, I don't remember doing it as an occasion of thoughtfulness. Maybe most people carry out their really heavy-duty thinking without being aware that that's what they're doing. But looking back, I see that my life turned in that little time-slice of Hazel and me sitting in silence with our trumpets correctly placed in waiting position.

If there were a photograph of us, "Carter Facing His First Life Crisis" would be my caption for the scene. I wasn't the musician I'd been thinking I was. Hazel Hicks was a much better trumpet player than I'd realized. And if Mr. White ever caught on to how good she was, he'd probably give her my chair.

Funny thing was, I kind of liked the way things were turning over in my mind. I'd found out Hazel's secret—that she was what I'd thought I was, the best musician in the band. And I was pretty sure she didn't realize that I'd figured it out from those four bars she'd played to demonstrate exactly how I hadn't gotten them right.

So I had her secret, and she probably didn't know I had it. I kind of savored that. But the other news that was coming to me was that I felt relieved of something heavy I hadn't realized I'd been carrying. I didn't have to be the best—and not just in band but in the whole school. I didn't have to be that kid anymore.

Okay, I looked at her, and I'm guessing what I wanted my face to tell her was that I appreciated her taking that load off my shoulders. She looked back at me—way longer than she'd ever looked at me before—and I had this rush of hoping that I would see that quick little smile of hers that I'd seen once or twice.

I hoped in vain. But while we were eye to eye with each other, I imagined that she wanted to smile at me and was just keeping the impulse under control. I admit this was probably deluded thinking. But what wasn't delusion was the blush that came up her neck and into her face. That blush is a historical fact.

After we passed through that cosmic time-out somebody had declared for us, we got back to business. Maybe the ghost of Vivaldi tapped his baton on the podium the way Mr. White did in band practice. We took up the second Allegro section. I set the count at the usual pace for our first time through.

That section is way tougher than the first one, and even though we played to the end, we both shook our heads when we finished and laughed at how terrible we sounded. I hadn't ever witnessed Hazel laughing at anything, and I was thrilled. I guess any time you're alone with somebody and you're both laughing, it's a sweet experience.

How things would have gone after that I can't say, though I can imagine that she and I might have extended the pleasure of laughing together. She said, very softly, "Slow the tempo next time?" But somebody knocked on the door to signal that our hour was over, and Hazel and I snapped back into our former selves.

We'd had our practice hour right after lunch, and we both had classes immediately afterward. I was carrying that hour with Hazel in my mind as I was slipping through the crowd in the hallway. I thought that in these hallways she was probably the same person she'd always been, but I was different. Lighter!

Habit carried me through the days that followed. From back in middle school I've been a talker, a chatter, a greeter, a shoulder- or arm- or back-toucher—a friendly guy, most people would have said of me. I hadn't realized that my talky ways were a constant song I sang at school and even at home with my Mom and Dad and little sister.

Stepping down from the pedestal on which I'd put myself didn't change my behavior. If anything it authenticated me—I wasn't trying to prove how cool and friendly I was, I had no agenda. Turns out I really liked these kids I'd been glad-handing all this time. So to my ear the constant song of my school days had started sounding real.

I haven't mentioned my girlfriends—Fay Tomlinson and Judy Crockett. They were pals with each other, and they liked to say they enjoyed sharing me. People made threesome jokes about us, not always the nicest jokes either, but we didn't care. We went to parties and dances. We even had special Carter-Judy-Fay dance moves we liked to show off.

All right, yes, sometimes we did some making out and petting, the three of us, but we didn't seek out opportunities for that. We weren't sexually adventurous. We liked being with a bunch of people. The conversations we had were not deep. I think we knew that if we really got to know each other, that might be the end of us.

Fay and Judy were like me—friendly, extroverted, in no hurry to couple up. We sometimes pointed out two kids splitting off from the general flow, leaving dances and parties early, holding hands in the hallways, nuzzling up beside their lockers. Occasionally we teased each other about "having an interest" in this person or that one.

I should say straight off that I never thought of Hazel Hicks as a potential girlfriend. I felt no romantic or sexual buzz when I thought about her. I don't think I "liked" her, but I did think about her a lot. I liked it that she'd made me see through myself. I liked it that she most likely didn't know what she'd done for me.

Our next practice hour was on a Monday after I'd worked pretty hard on the Vivaldi at home. I didn't do this to prove to Hazel that I was better than she was, but I definitely wanted to show her that I could be "professional" about our recital.

Do you really aspire to be a grown-up when you're in high

school? Me, I'd aspired to be a cool guy for so long I didn't quite know what to try for now that I'd seen through my cool-guy routines. I must have been in some middle territory between being a kid and being a grown-up. It takes a certain kind of kid to be a "professional."

I was a little late getting to the room, but not so much that I felt I needed to apologize. Hazel already had our music set up on our stands, and she was just starting to warm up when I stepped in. I confess that I gave her the once-over while she was standing with her back to me, pointing her trumpet toward the far corner.

Straight brown hair cut to just above her shoulder, white blouse tucked into a navy blue skirt, nondescript flats, no make-up, no jewelry except for a funny-looking silver ring she wore on her left thumb. She probably had her eyes closed while she was warming up—she almost always did. Neither appealing nor unappealing was my conclusion.

Basic human being was how she presented herself. And I admired that. Why it should have pleased me that she tried to be so generic I can't say. I can say that it might have been the first real opinion I'd ever had that was all my own. Nobody else would see Hazel as I did. Well, to put it bluntly—nobody else would see her. Period.

When we sat down to practice we were like-minded. We went through the first movement at a ridiculously slow tempo. When we finished, I said it sounded childish, and she nodded. We worked on a couple of phrases that were troublesome. Then we played at tempo, and when we finished we looked at each other and I got the smile.

I could say, with some truth, that my life was complete in the exact moment of Hazel's little three-second lopsided grin. I couldn't help giving her my own happy face, and mine was just about as short-lived as hers.

When we set to work on the second movement we seemed to know what we were doing. We took it at a slow tempo and stopped whenever we hit a rough patch. I was relieved to hear a couple of flaws in her attacks and a phrase that she rushed. We were saying hardly anything and when we did speak it was *yes, here, no, stop,* and *okay.*

After a while we were so deep in the composition and the two of us were so closely aligned in our struggle with it that it was like studying old Vivaldi as a philosopher of some kind. And we were getting somewhere! Hazel actually tapped the music at bar 22 of the second movement and whispered, "Happy here." I nodded like crazy.

When the knock on the door came, it felt wrong that we had to give up the room. Neither Hazel nor I spoke to the kids whose turn it was to practice, and we didn't even say goodbye to each other. But after I got over my pouting—which was about halfway through Mrs. Simmerman's boring World History class, my good spirits came back to me.

We were signed up for the room for two more sessions. In the next one Mr. White would check us out to tell us what we needed to work on to be ready for the recital. I wasn't worried about what he'd say about our playing the Vivaldi piece, but I was concerned that maybe he'd figure out what I had, that Hazel was a stronger player than I was.

I actually thought I'd be okay with his giving her the first chair of the first trumpets and demoting me to the second trumpet section. I already knew my response to anybody who'd ask me about it—"She's better than me." And I'd shrug and say, "What can I say?" What I thought would really hurt was seeing his disappointment in me.

Mr. White had been in the Air Force band. He was tall, charismatic, demanding, and temperamental. Once he'd stepped down off the podium to yell at Susan Short, our oboist, for playing too softly, and he'd tapped her stomach with his fingers and shouted, "From the gut, Susan!" And Susan Short was the prettiest girl in the band.

My own father could have cared less what chair I had in the band—he appreciated my good grades and my being vice-president of my class. He liked to put his arm around me and say that I was his ticket to the easy life when he got old. He never said so, but I'm pretty sure he thought being in the band and playing trumpet was a waste of time.

Hazel and I got lucky and had the practice room to ourselves for the first fifteen minutes or so of our hour. I think we were both feeling pretty good about where we were with the concerto. We warmed up as usual, but just from the scales and riffs she played, I could tell Hazel was looking forward to showing Mr. White what we could do.

When we took our seats, I got a bright idea and said, "Let's play this first movement in double-time and see what happens." She gave me a droll look but raised her trumpet, and I did set the count at a ridiculously fast pace. Miraculously we managed to do it. We turned a four-minute piece into a two-minute circus march for the clowns.

Maybe we would have broken into raucous laughter about it except that the minute we ripped out the last note, the door opened, and Mr. White stepped in. He gave us both his stink-eye, the look he reserved for kids who hadn't stopped talking when he was trying to explain something important. He shook his head at us and said, "I don't want to know."

Then he scooted a chair over to the corner, sat down, and said, "When you're ready." My heart was a jackhammer, but something made me raise my mouthpiece to my lips as if we had to play the piece right that instant. A light touch on my elbow made me turn slightly toward Hazel. She held her horn on her lap, and she was looking straight into my face.

I lowered my trumpet, but I kept returning her look, and I don't know how she communicated this, but all of a sudden I knew I had to take some deep breaths. We stared at each other a while longer, and when she turned her head to the music, my heart had settled down, I was calm and happy. Without looking I felt her nod, and I murmured the count.

The three descending quarter notes that start the piece seemed to come from a single source somewhere between the bells of our two trumpets. Whoever was playing that single instrument must have been personally acquainted with the composer. I knew it must have been Hazel and I who were responsible, but I'd never heard us sound so sublime.

I snuck a look at Mr. White about a minute into the first section. His eyes were closed, and he was swaying in his chair. He had a sort of smile on his face, and that made me even happier. Then I thought of him jabbing Susan Short's solar plexus with his fingers and yelling, "From the gut, Susan," and that made me happier still.

Mr. White swaying with his eyes closed and my remembering Susan Short made me think of Vivaldi. I'd read that he taught at an orphanage for especially talented girls, and I could feel how the sound our trumpets were making must have come down to Hazel and me through Mr. White from girls who had played this concerto three hundred years ago.

Hazel and I were staring at each other, both of us completely aware that we'd gone beyond ourselves. The concerto seemed to have played us rather the other way around. Mr. White was staring wide-eyed at us. "Hazel! Carter!" he said. He was choked up. "You kids!" he said, blinking and shaking his head as he headed out the door.

Hazel and I were unable to say anything. We had no context for what we needed to do in order to re-enter our lives on the other side of that door. We put our horns back in their cases. Then we faced each other again. An embrace wasn't possible. But we did put our wet cheeks together. And in maybe fifteen seconds the knock at the door sounded.

First Chair, Second Trumpet: Part i

In this studio portrait, my Aunt Hazel is fourteen, she's standing at attention, and she has on her high school band uniform, which is cream colored with a dark chest panel with brass buttons and embroidered filigrees across the front. She has pulled her hair back in a ponytail. She holds her trumpet tucked against her side with the bell facing the photographer, and her face is both serious and bemused. When I showed her this picture, she said nothing, but she took it from me and just sat with it quietly. I watched her study it for some minutes, but then I noticed that her eyes weren't really directed toward the picture; she was gazing more or less across the room.

So evidently it had taken her back into her memories of being in that band. Other pictures I'd showed her she always handed back pretty quickly, but I wasn't sure she was going to let me have this one back. Though she wore glasses and her face was that of an old person, I could have sworn her expression was the same as that of the girl in the photograph. So I kept my voice soft—I didn't want to disturb her reverie—and I asked her what she could tell me about the photograph. "Oh, John Robert," she said with a softness to match mine, "I could tell you so much about those days that we'd be sitting here all afternoon."

I waited for her to go on. I'd learned she preferred to find her own way into whatever she was going to tell me. "This picture was taken not long after I'd started playing that horn and gotten into the band. It was the one period of my life when everything seemed sort of perfect. Our band director was new in town, and he was a very charismatic man who told me I had some ability as a trumpet player. Maybe he told all the kids that, because he was eager for our band to be the biggest our town had ever seen. But he was the first person who'd ever flattered me. About anything."

She faced me and said very quietly, "I don't know if you know this, John Robert, but as a child I was a real loner, and here this man had me playing music and marching with a hundred other kids who were just as excited about it as I was. Being in that band made me feel like wings had sprouted out of my back and suddenly I could fly. You know those flocks of starlings that you see making fantastic patterns in the sky around twilight? I was like one of them—not just in the marching, but in the music we played. So in my mind, my body, my senses, my whole self, I had this powerful sense of belonging."

First Chair, Second Trumpet: Part II

When I returned the next morning, the band picture was still on Aunt Hazel's kitchen table. She poured us both cups of tea, and I didn't even have to ask her a question. She told me that looking at that photograph had opened up a chapter of her life that she must have closed years ago. "I'm not a social person, John Robert, you know that about me. But in the band kids were friendly to me and I was around people I admired for their ability as musicians. And for their seriousness. I'd thought it was only adults who were serious, which was what made them not much fun to be around.

"I knew some middle-schoolers who were serious about getting good grades, but that was because they were under pressure from their parents. But somebody my age who'd practice a single piece of music for hours and hours every day? A kid who loved doing something that was difficult because he loved it? I hadn't witnessed that before, and I wanted to be that kind of person. I wanted to play my trumpet the way Mousey Spence played his, making a sound that almost made me cry. At thirteen and fourteen years old I was a scatterbrained idiot, but I had the capacity to recognize elegance and passion when another kid made it come out of a horn.

"Chimer Durham, who was a couple of years older than me and a real jerk, nevertheless had the ability to play the piccolo solo in *Stars and Stripes Forever* with such exuberance it would make you want to do a jig." Aunt Hazel paused a moment, staring into her teacup like it was the portal back to her years as a high school musician. "I still don't know what to think of those days," she murmured. "I was a child then, and most of us in that band were children, but the music raised us up to something we couldn't have imagined. Mr. White, the band director, was a gifted teacher, and I give him credit—he knew how to turn us children into grown-ups the instant he tapped the podium with his baton and we raised our horns to our mouths. He could do that.

"But it was the music that taught us the deeper aptitudes—respect for the work it took to become a musician, admiration for the talent that enabled a few of us to create art with our instruments. I didn't think about any of that back then. A thirteen-year-old isn't a thoughtful creature. I just knew I loved every minute I spent with those kids in that band. A few of them were sort of my friends, and a few of them I didn't care for, but mostly we were all just band-mates. We were young, but we could do something we knew to be of value. There are plenty of grown-ups in this town and all over the planet who will never know what that's like."

NONE

1964 — Burlington, Vermont

ej

HAZEL HICKS WAS THE FIRST "NONE" TO GRADUATE CROSS-
ley State College as a Religion Major. Hazel herself thought this
was nothing special. She thought it an obvious choice for someone like her. Which is to say, a person who took every form of life
seriously but who found all creation stories implausible—even
the most entertaining and compelling.

With the exception of science, of course. Hazel accepted
Science not as *the truth*, but as *the most likely truth*. Even Science, bless its earnest heart, could not explain giraffes. Or beetles,
hummingbirds, whales, or monarch butterflies. In her opinion,
Genesis and evolution were both struggling to tell the same impossible story.

Hazel respected evolution, but it made her smile and shake
her head. Which was her response as a little girl to the Bible's account of the great flood, Noah's ark, the animals two by two, the
dove, and the rainbow. Ten-year-old Hazel couldn't get enough
of that story. She also liked the Garden of Eden, Adam and Eve,
the apple, and the serpent.

Those stories commanded the child Hazel's attention, though
she never "believed" them for a second. She didn't say so at the
time, but she thought believing them wasn't the point and it was

stupid to take them that way. Which was the kind of child Hazel was. Which made grown-ups wary of her. Even her parents often found her hard to take.

Science had nothing like those old stories, which nineteen-year-old Hazel thought was sad. Smiling and shaking her head was her rueful acknowledgment that what science had to say about the extraordinary and incessant panorama of life on the planet Earth could not replace the childish pleasure she had taken from the old biblical narratives.

The gap between science and what she supposed she had to call faith was what "required"—her word—Hazel to declare Religion as her major and "None" as her religious preference. But when she graduated she couldn't find a job. One interviewer chuckled at her and said, "Well Ms. Hicks, you're kind of a misfit, aren't you?"

ℰℜ

When she couldn't get a real job after she graduated, she worked a summer for the city of Burlington as a parking lot attendant. She kept applying for other jobs, but she had no luck and felt humiliated. Remembering she'd graduated Magna Cum Laude from Crossley made her eyes go teary. At the end of August, Ms. Hicks became a school bus driver.

Her supervisor had pity on her and assigned her one of the new buses, which had automatic transmission and a nice smell. On her first day of training she thought they might fire her because she drove so cautiously. The size of the thing intimidated her. But her instructor was patient, and by the last training day, she'd gotten her confidence.

Pete Hoofnagle had driven school buses for the city for fifty years. He knew all the routes. He sat shotgun—front seat to the driver's right—for her practice run. Pete had gone to grade school with her mom. At the end of the run he told Ms. Hicks, "Your mother couldn't drive a bus if her life depended on it. Don't tell her I said so."

Pete's words made her blush with pleasure at the time, and she knew she'd remember them in the months to come. Truth was, Ms. Hicks was a little ashamed of her job. She'd have liked working for a newspaper, a TV station, a magazine, a social services department, even a church. After she had the bus to herself that day, she sat in it a long while.

Dr. Norsworthy, who'd taught her "Philosophic Questions and Religious Response," had been her favorite professor at Crossley. He was generally gruff but his tone changed as he answered her questions in class. When she'd challenged him over Bonhoeffer's concept of obedience, he'd answered her for ten minutes and with passion ringing in his voice.

Alone in her assigned school bus, Ms. Hicks composed a letter she knew she would never write or send to Dr. Norsworthy. She would tell him that she was ashamed of being ashamed of her new job. She would tell him that if she could stand the job for ten months, it would be because of his answer to her question about Bonhoeffer and obedience.

&

Rachel and Nick King were her first passengers. Their mother was out there with them when Hazel stopped, but she didn't step up to the bus door to introduce the children. She gave Hazel a quick smile before turning back to their house. The Kings didn't send their children to college, but people in the Five Sisters neighborhood respected them.

Rachel's dress and sweater were new. Nick's shirt was freshly ironed, and his jeans had that new stiff-as-boards look to them. Hazel wasn't used to seeing children so early in the morning.

These King kids were still sleepy. Hazel's roster told her Rachel was eleven and Nick nine. Rachel sat right up front, Nick walked three rows back.

Hazel hadn't thought about how she would get along with the children who rode her bus, and she was surprised at how interested she was in Rachel and Nick King. That happened with the Hester twins, too. Unlike the King children, Phil and Pete Hester were wide awake, and their sly faces suggested not serious trouble but definitely mischief.

Dear Dr. Norsworthy, "Obedience" may not be just a personal issue. I may have to decide how to apply or not apply it to the elementary school children who ride my bus. I know you consider my secular version of obedience to be just a homegrown form of "cheap grace." But how might you and Bonhoeffer advise me to deal with ten-year-old heathens?

When the three Dunford children and Buntsy Williams boarded her bus, Hazel realized she was inordinately attentive to her passengers. She concentrated on trying to "read" these children as she had learned to read texts in her Crossan seminar. Their faces were so astonishingly forthcoming and compelling they seemed to command her to study them.

As more children boarded, Hazel found herself overwhelmed by their personal data—their clothes, their voices, their shoes, their teeth, how they smelled, their likelihood of failure or success. Nothing in Hazel's upbringing or education had prepared her for having her mind and her heart stuffed with her impressions of so many children.

ご

They became "her children." But only in a very limited sense. It was easy enough to speak of them to her family as "her passengers"—that was the public truth. But "her children" was how Hazel thought of them when she was alone. Her private truth.

When she was carrying out what Dr. Norsworthy would have called "her spiritual reckoning."

Brunhilde Copenhaver, a.k.a. Pruney, an overweight third-grader, was clearly in crisis mode that first morning as she climbed the steps up into the bus. Hazel would have discerned that much even if Pruney hadn't shown her a panic-filled face. She was a child passing through the gates of hell. A child who knew torture would be her fate.

Pruney had a history, of course, and Hazel couldn't do anything about that. But she could—and did—stop Tim Lewis and Bobby Joe Branscomb from pulling Pruney's hair, pinching her, and calling her Jiggles and Jello Butt. Hazel pulled the bus over slightly, stopped and walked back to where Tim and Bobby Joe sat, grinning, waiting for her.

She put her face very close to theirs. "I will tell your parents." She spoke quietly. "If you touch her or say anything else to her." She looked each boy in the eyes until he turned away. Hazel had older brothers, nicer boys than these two, but of the same species. Hazel wasn't afraid of them. She knew how to make a boy afraid of her.

Pete Hoofnagle heard what she'd done and waited for her at school a couple of mornings later. "You're not supposed to stop the bus like that," he told her. Hazel was reading his face and his voice. She knew he'd say more. "But when you do, I advise you to put on your blinkers." He winked at her and turned away. "Thank you," she called to his back.

Kate and Joanne Delby, Wilmer Pope, James Shinault, and Betty Tomlinson, all of them decent kids, quietly did their homework on the bus in the mornings, then going home jabbered and hollered like baboons. Hazel liked those children though she often had to ask them to quiet down. They'd do what she asked, at least for a little while.

&

Dr. Norsworthy, I'm reading Merton. Did you know that he polished floors and scrubbed dishes while he was waiting to find out if they would let him into the monastery? I can't help thinking my school-bus driving days are a test for something I'm suited for. I don't know what. Yes, my answer to the religious preference question is still None.

At the beginning of October, Hazel realized she had become friends with Rachel King. Rachel sat in that shotgun seat from her first day on Hazel's bus, and she'd invited Pruney Copenhaver to sit with her regularly. But Pruney was quiet and morose, whereas Rachel was such a chatterbox that every day she spilled out hundreds of details about her life.

Hazel would have never chosen Rachel as her friend, and she was sure Rachel wasn't even aware of how close she and Hazel were. Hazel shook her head when she thought about how intimate they'd become without either of them meaning to do so. Rachel was smart only in a scatterbrained kind of way, but Hazel respected her anyway.

And Rachel was truly and completely just a kid. Hazel could see that Rachel had breasts but she hadn't had a period, she said she hated boys, she still slept with her Teddy bear, and *Little House on the Prairie* was the most grown-up book she'd read. Also, even though she constantly asked Hazel questions, she only half-listened to what Hazel told her.

Hazel worried that she "ingested" too much information about the kids on her bus in general and about Rachel in particular. She couldn't help what she learned from simply being their witness for a couple of hours each day. But why did she have to lose sleep over Rachel's mother letting the child eat Pringles instead of vegetables or fruit?

One day Rachel rushed up beside Hazel walking through the school parking lot, hugged her awkwardly and fiercely, proclaimed, "I just love you, Ms. Hicks!" then skipped away to catch up with her friends. Hazel understood the act as spontaneous, but that didn't help her process the sensation of that girl's body flying without warning into her arms.

✑

It startled Hazel to think that maybe Rachel felt about her as she felt about Dr. Norsworthy. She could think of many ways in which it wasn't the same. It made her cringe to imagine giving her professor a hug of the sort that Rachel had given her. But he'd made her understand that he took her seriously. Wasn't that what she'd done with Rachel?

Benny Sutphin, the new boy, began riding Ms. Hicks's bus in mid-October. He got on with Franklin Hoback, though neither boy was friendly with the other. Hazel stopped Benny from heading down the aisle—she actually extended her arm to prevent him from passing—and insisted that he tell her his name before she let him take a seat.

Benny was twelve, which made him one of the oldest children at Fork Mountain Elementary. He slouched, he had zits and facial hair, and he had a smell Ms. Hicks was pretty sure was cologne. He wouldn't look directly at her, he didn't like her sticking her arm out to stop him, didn't like her making him tell her both his first and last names.

When Benny muttered that first morning, Ms. Hicks had to ask him to repeat himself, which he definitely didn't like. When the boy glanced at her then and noticed her smiling at him, his jaw tightened, and his eyes became slits. What she thought she saw—grown-up rage—was real enough to send a shiver through her. *No more smiles for him*, she decided.

Before Benny, Hazel hadn't realized how much she used the big mirror over her windshield to read the children's faces and body language. Now when Benny stepped up into the bus, she watched the kids responding to him as he walked toward the back. Nobody looked straight at him or spoke to him. They all went quiet. The girls lowered their eyes.

Ms. Hicks hoped Benny would find his place among the children on her bus. He was skinny and small for a boy of twelve, and he was mildly hostile, but he wasn't a bully. The kids would eventually have taken him in if he'd allowed it. Somebody would have befriended him. But they seemed to understand he wanted nothing to do with any of them.

℃

The Wednesday before Thanksgiving, Hazel and her mother made a list of the groceries they needed. Then Hazel took the family car to do the shopping while her mother prepared the house for her brothers' homecoming. They'd arrive Thursday afternoon and stay through Sunday. This would be Hazel's first grown-up Thanksgiving. She was no longer a student.

In the two and a half months she'd been a driver, she'd begun to enjoy doing her job well. She liked the details of carrying out the maintenance on the bus, cleaning it up in the evenings, and sticking to her schedule so that the kids and their parents could depend on her being on time. She had proved to herself that she was a capable person.

She wished she felt better about helping her mother with Thanksgiving this year. It wasn't much different from the previous ones. From sixth or seventh grade on, she'd enjoyed helping and talking with her mother while they prepared the food. By her senior year in high school the two of them behaved like sisters when they were in the kitchen.

But this year Hazel couldn't shake off her awareness that she still lived at home. After college her brothers had moved away and found their own places to live. Throughout the fall her mother had said things like "Honey, I'm just glad you have a job" and "Your father and I love having you here." But her whole family knew she was—well, what?

Underachieving was the term they'd use if she were in high school or college. And they'd call her overqualified for being a school bus driver when she'd been a Magna Cum Laude college graduate. She helped her mother pick up the turkey and set it down in the big cooler full of brining mixture. Something about the naked turkey carcass made Hazel weepy.

Her mother noticed but said nothing. If she understood what was wrong with Hazel, Hazel wished she'd let her in on the secret. Her mother plopped herself down at the kitchen table, announced that she was exhausted, and asked Hazel if she'd mind fixing the cornbread. "I'll tell you how," she said. Hazel nodded. Moving her hands made her feel okay.

℮〻

Ms. Hicks ordinarily said good morning to each of her children as they stepped up onto her bus, and they wished her good morning as well. Some returned her greeting with enthusiasm, some murmured shyly, and a few grunted and moved past her with their minds on other matters. Benny Sutphin made no reply and pretended she didn't exist.

Hazel had stopped composing letters she wouldn't send to Dr. Norsworthy, but she couldn't stop wishing he could know about her job as a school bus driver. She wished she could talk with him about Rachel and Benny—a silly notion, she thought, because even though he'd been her academic advisor, she'd never discussed her personal life with him.

Benny's ignoring her and her good mornings brought her to the revelation that she knew nothing whatsoever about Dr. Norsworthy's life beyond his office and his classroom. *He never invited that kind of interest,* her mind instantly reminded her. *He was a professional. He'd have been embarrassed if I'd asked about his wife. If he had one.*

It was like her, she thought, to get herself worked up over something that existed only in her mind. Maybe Rachel had a thought about her every now and then, and Benny couldn't help hearing her pleasant greeting every school morning, but Dr. Norsworthy probably wouldn't remember her if she stood right in front of him and reminded him of her name.

But her mind, her relentlessly yammering, hand-wringing brain, wouldn't allow her to throw herself in a ditch of self-pity. *You greet each of these children every morning—even the hostile one—and you dispatch a generous thought to every one of them. For some of them yours are very likely the only pleasant looks they will receive all day.*

Dr. Norsworthy was of less and less help in her thinking. Dietrich Bonhoeffer was too heroic and too lofty to advise her on how to deal with ten-year-old heathens. Thomas Merton had washed dishes and scrubbed floors, but he'd had a goal in mind, a vocation to which he aspired. What did Hazel Hicks have beyond a job driving a school bus?

∽

One particular December morning Ms. Hicks noticed changes all around her. A light snow had fallen, the chill in the air was more like winter than like fall, and the trees had a hunkered-down look. Her bus had to make an extra chug before the engine started, and Hazel herself felt unusually alert for no reason she could figure out.

Rachel and Nick were rosy-cheeked and full of chatter about the puppy they hoped to get as a Christmas present. The Dunford kids were quarreling among themselves, and Buntsy Williams was whistling the first three bars of "Rudolph" over and over, so that Hazel had to ask him to stop. Pruney Copenhaver gave Hazel a look of desperate sadness.

Frank Hoback's face seemed to want to convey something to Hazel, but when Benny Sutphin climbed the steps staring straight at her, she wasn't ready for what she saw. His right eye was swollen nearly shut, and the flesh around it was visibly bruised. She thought she knew exactly what his outraged face meant to tell her. *Look what happened to me!*

"Oh, Benny," she murmured—and knew instantly that her pitying tone was wrong. He made a sound that was the human version of a wolf snarling and turned away. In the mirror she watched him heading for the back of the bus. She was pretty sure he was looking straight at each kid in turn as he passed by them, just daring them to say a word to him.

She considered turning the bus around and delivering all the children back to their homes. But she started the bus moving and thought hard about Benny. She moaned softly. Then she almost laughed aloud imagining her trio of great minds, Norsworthy, Bonhoeffer, and Merton, trying to advise her on what she should do about the boy.

The children spoke so quietly among themselves that the bus seemed to be sounding a minor chord. When she parked it and opened the door, the kids were eager to be free. Benny was the last to walk up the aisle. She raised her hand to let him know she wanted to speak to him. When she said his name, he slashed her arm with a pocketknife.

⁂

Hazel hadn't decided what she was going to say to Benny, and Benny probably hadn't decided what he was going to do until the instant he did it. The boy moved past her quickly and when his feet hit the asphalt surface of the parking lot, he started running—in the opposite direction of school. Hazel watched him and held her arm tightly.

When she couldn't see him anymore, she looked down to see how seriously he'd injured her. Blood was showing on her jacket, which meant it had seeped through her blouse and sweater. Her arm ached, so she knew the cut was deep and she'd have to go for stitches. She looked up and saw Rachel and Pruney staring up at her through the open door.

"Are you okay?" Rachel's face was pale. "Not so much," Hazel told her. "Will you girls step back up here a minute and help me?" As they moved up the steps, Ms. Hicks asked Pruney if she might use her scarf. "I'll buy you a new one," she said. Of the two girls, Pruney seemed calmest, and so Hazel asked her to wind the scarf around the arm.

While Pruney did the winding—with surprising steadiness—Rachel averted her eyes. "What happened?" she asked. Hazel wanted to pat her friend on the shoulder and tell her everything was going to be fine. What she did say was, "You don't want to know, sweetheart." She asked the girls not to tell anyone what they had seen or that she was hurt.

"I want you to go to Mr. Hoofnagle's office and tell him to meet me at the emergency room," she told them. They nodded with such trusting faces that Hazel thought she might start weeping. "Only Mr. Hoofnagle. Don't tell anybody else anything," she said. "Cross your hearts and hope to die?" All three crossed their hearts, Hazel with her left hand.

Driving the empty bus to the hospital, Hazel pondered the heart-crossing ritual. Didn't the vow require an obvious lie? *Who would ever hope to die and mean it?* She drove with her left hand on the steering wheel and her right hand in her lap. She was grateful for the bus's automatic transmission because she didn't have to change gears.

Hazel thought she got off easy—twenty stitches, a tetanus shot, and a couple of hours in the emergency room. Best of all was the young doctor who didn't press her for details. He asked her what had happened, of course, and when she told him she didn't want to say, he nodded. "Boyfriend, huh?" he said. Hazel shrugged and tried to look ashamed.

When Pete Hoofnagle stepped through the curtain and sat down beside her, she had to stifle her weeping impulse. He touched the hand of her injured arm, but he kept quiet. They had almost no privacy in the little curtained off area. It took Hazel a while to speak, and she didn't even try to tell him how grateful she was that he'd arrived.

To tell the story, she had to whisper with him leaning close. He made soft noises in his chest and visibly flinched when she told him how hard Benny's knife had struck her arm. "You're the only person beside Benny and me who knows what happened," she said. "I need you to promise you won't tell anybody else." He blinked at her.

They were interrupted by the nurse giving Hazel her prescriptions, the instructions for caring for the wound, and the card with her follow-up appointment. On the way out to her bus, Pete walked closely beside her, and he followed her up the steps. She took the driver's seat, and he sat shotgun, as he had during her training runs.

He cleared his throat. "I think you should report the incident and press charges," he said. These were the first words he'd spoken to her. Hazel told him she knew that's what he'd think. Pete gave her what he probably intended to be a grin and said, "I know you're not likely to take my advice." She watched him doing his best to read her face.

Hazel thought it was peculiar she knew Pete as well as she

did. He'd probably spoken no more than a hundred words to her altogether. Then she realized that when they were sitting on this bus, each of them understood the other very well. She knew he felt duty bound to try to persuade her to do what he very well knew she was not going to do.

♋

"It'll be hard for you to keep this to yourself," Pete said. "I have to tell you the kid's likely to hurt somebody else if you let him get by with this." Hazel's mind brought up Benny's face the instant after he'd struck her. His black eye was nearly swollen shut, but his good eye was wildly open. *That boy needed to see that I realized he'd hurt me.*

Pete wouldn't say any more until she responded. But she couldn't seem to make herself let go of how Benny's body had looked when he grabbed the post and swiveled down out of the bus—like he'd learned to fly. And she'd had to watch him running across the parking lot and down Fork Mountain Road. She'd watched until she couldn't see him anymore.

"But maybe not," she said softly. Until she said this, she hadn't put the feeling into words. "Maybe he won't want to do anything like this ever again." Pete's face told her he thought she might be an idiot. She had a little burst of knowing he could be right. Dr. Norsworthy, Merton, Bonhoeffer, and even her mom might think so, too.

"The decision he made to do that to you"—Pete raised his hand in the direction of her bandaged arm—"will make it all the easier for him next time he gets mad." He waited. Hazel knew better than to argue. So he went on. "If he does hurt another person, you'll hate yourself." His voice was quiet. He'd come to the end of what he had to say.

Exhaustion descended on Hazel so hard and so suddenly she thought she'd have to pass out or start crying. She opened her mouth to tell Pete she couldn't think about any of it anymore, she was too woozy. In the seats behind them she felt the Dunford kids, Buntsy Williams, the Hester twins, Franklin Hoback, Rachel and Nick King, Pruney Copenhaver and her torturers Tim Lewis and Bobby Joe Branscomb, Kate and Joanne Delby, Wilmer Pope, James Shinault, and Betty Tomlinson, all those decent kids staring out their windows, in the trance of riding to school or riding back home.

They'd all been there this morning, and they'd be there tomorrow morning, too. But right now Pete was waiting for her. "You'll help me, won't you?" Hazel could barely make herself say the words. Pete blinked. "If Benny hurts somebody else. If I start to hate myself?" Pete flinched and kept quiet, but his face gave her the answer anyway.

Group Picture with the Middle-School Children who Rode Her Bus

This is the picture she used to show me when I was in middle school. My parents would drop me off at her house so they could have a weekend to themselves. Aunt Hazel and I both loved those occasions, and it never occurred to me that there was anything unusual about a boy spending a couple of nights with his unmarried aunt. She took me out for treats and lunch, she took me to the movies, she took me out on the lake in a canoe, and she made popcorn for me in her old stove-top popcorn popper—then when I turned eleven, she let me shake that old popper, which at the time was a really exciting thing to do.

This photograph shows her standing in front of her school bus with twelve or thirteen middle-school children on either side of her. What she and I both craved to do was for me to pick out a boy or girl then for her to tell me everything she knew about that kid. She had stories to tell about all of them. They were more or less my age, and I could have fit just fine in that picture with them, but of course they were strangers to me. At least they were until she told me about them. Aunt Hazel and I were both surprised that I could usually remember their names after she'd talked about them.

Pruney Copenhaver was so completely a snob that she didn't mind being teased about it. Rachel King was the smartest kid my Aunt Hazel ever met until I came along. Joe Branscomb was girl crazy. Kate Delby actually got into a fistfight with Buntsy Williams. And Benny Sutphin wasn't in the picture, which made him all the more fascinating to me. He'd slashed my Aunt Hazel's arm with a pocketknife, he'd run away from home the same day, and when the sheriff had finally caught up with him, they took him to jail and then put him in a foster home. Aunt Hazel hadn't seen him since the day he slashed her arm, but she'd describe him again and again, like she was trying to make him real in her mind:

"Benny slouched, he had zits and a few little sprigs of facial hair. He also had this smell that just had to be cologne, and it was so strong he must have put it on just before he left his house to catch the school bus." Every time we looked at the picture, she tried to explain him to me. "I saw that he had a black eye that morning when he got on the bus. If I'd had my wits about me, I'd have known he was looking for trouble. If I'd been a little smarter about him, maybe he wouldn't have cut my arm." She'd shake her head. I knew she felt responsible for what happened to Benny, but I knew there wasn't anything I could tell her that would make her feel better about it. Also I loved to hear her tell his story.

HOW HAZEL TRIED TO KILL
THE ONE GOOD THING

1969 — New York City, Upper West Side

ભ

HAZEL NEVER COMPLETELY MOVED INTO FORREST'S APARTMENT.
She kept paying her rent in graduate housing, but she left more
and more of her clothes, shampoo, shoes, and books, etc., at his
place. Forrest made it easy for her to forget she had her own bed.
He was an early riser, but he preferred that she sleep in, so that
he could bring her morning coffee to her. Sometimes he'd slip
under the covers and invite her to snuggle with him while he read
the newspaper to her.

For a man who was a genius of comical newspaper reading
aloud while snuggling in bed, Forrest's looks were hard to take
until you got used to him. Which in her case took a while. When
she first saw him, the proportions of his face seemed so horrify-
ingly wrong that she thought she couldn't bear to talk with him.
His nose, forehead, and cheekbones looked like Picasso had sur-
gically rearranged them when he was a baby—Picasso despairing
over the human condition.

What happened to you? was the question that kept recurring
to her when they finally did end up talking. She didn't ask it out
loud, but it took some willpower. They were in the West End

Bar on Broadway—a place they and their grad school friends went on weekend evenings. A brainless place, as she remembers it now. Evidently that's what they both were looking for in their mid-twenties. You had to shout to be heard unless you wanted to stand really close.

What did they talk about? Their parents? God yes, the memory makes her cringe. Forrest had had an army colonel for a father and a mean drunk for a mother. He'd grown up mostly at Fort Campbell, Kentucky. Hazel's father was a mid-level manager for Union Carbide, and her mother had taught high school art. Their idea of a wild time was a glass of Mogen David wine when her father came home from work. Hazel has always been stupidly ashamed of them.

"Hey," Forrest had shouted, "I'll trade parents with you any time. I'll even throw in some uncles and aunts if you're in the market for screwed-up relatives." It wasn't so much what he said as the way his mutilated face—even in the act of shouting—conveyed solidarity with her. And the way he took half a step closer to her, placed his arm feather-light over her shoulder and tried to speak softly. When she brings that moment back, it just about kills her.

Maybe she should have asked him. *What's wrong with your face.* Most likely his answer would have been, *Nothing, I was just born this way.* He wouldn't have been offended. He might even have been amused. After they'd become so caught up in each other that they spent every possible hour together—and this took months because Hazel couldn't stop stifling her feelings—she glanced at Forrest one morning and had to catch her breath he was so fine-looking.

He was slouched in his reading chair by his apartment's bay window that looked out on West End Avenue; she was on her way to the shower around 8 A.M. of a January morning. He had on a heavy wool sweater, he needed a shave, his thick hair was a mess, and he was so engrossed in what he was reading that he didn't notice her walking on her bare feet from the bedroom to the bathroom. A shaft of edgy winter sunlight had fallen over him. She stopped and stood still.

The young man was illuminated like an angel in a 16th century painting, though no painter with whom she was acquainted could have done justice to the tableau. His face was the issue—it still had that brutish structure. *Well,* she made herself admit as she studied him, *that's a wreck of a face, no doubt about it.* But what the light accomplished was to reveal the extraordinarily sweet spirit that lay just beneath Forrest's thick nose and heavy brows.

Hazel couldn't make herself stop seeing the ugliness, but this ruthless light washing over him insisted she see both at once—the ruined and the radiant. She knew Forrest's thoughts were far away from this worldly moment in which she stood gazing at him. It would embarrass him to catch her ogling him, but she had no intention of moving until she'd finished feasting on the sight of him. *How I want that man!* She shook her head to try to make it not so.

But it was so, and no amount of head-shaking would free her from the current of desire sweeping her toward some destination she couldn't even imagine. Later the question would come to her, *What does recognizing the physical beauty of another person have to do with genitalia and body fluids and the bizarre mechanics of mating? Or why does the one call forth the other?* About those issues Hazel continued shaking her head for some months. To no avail.

While she stood frozen in her contemplation of Forrest, his eyes shifted upward from the page of his book to her face. Just before she noted that infinitesimal change in him, she'd become aware of the old blue nightgown she had on. It was the only one she owned that could keep her warm in his cold apartment, but it had a ripped shoulder and its former bluebell blue had faded into dirty-sidewalk gray. She'd caught the musty scent and knew it needed washing.

Hazel wasn't one of those young women whose first thought about almost anything was *What should I wear?*, but right then, as Forrest's eyes locked into hers, she really wished her appearance was better than she knew it to be. For one thing she was certain she had a severe case of bed-head that, along with the confederate-widow nightgown, probably made her look like an inmate in a mental-health institution. Forrest didn't look away. Neither did she.

From her mid-teens Hazel had practiced what she now thought of as Subjunctive Theology. She believed in science. But she also knew that intricate currents of mystery constantly wafting through her life had made her invent a creator that possessed thoughts and feelings like a human being. She liked to think this creator regarded human antics with transcendent objectivity. And wouldn't omniscience make you have a pretty good sense of humor?

In Forrest's West End Avenue apartment that morning she sensed the two of them regarding each other with a human kind of detachment. She'd not only forgiven him his disarranged face, she'd comprehended that his might be the loveliest face she'd ever see. She shuddered to think maybe she'd just discovered love. But then she couldn't help fearing what Forrest's objective gaze might be making of her. He could be seeing a complete mess of a woman.

Her witty creator might think it amusing that in her moment of realizing love, the object of her affection suddenly found her repulsive. She shuddered even harder. She'd always suspected that if another person could truly see her, that person might just start puking. Hazel had often noted that she was hateful, judgmental, selfish, ungenerous, self-centered, mentally limited, spiritually rotten, and altogether a stinking wad of protoplasm.

When she was on a roll of self-loathing, Hazel could generate considerable momentum. In her bare feet and stinking nightgown she was poised to start one of her falls from self-esteem. But the moment slowed. She turned into a big rock with eyeballs. She watched Forrest's expression slowly soften from objectivity toward whatever its opposite was. Probably not love but maybe desire. Maybe affection, she thought. Something really hot but probably not love.

Starting that morning they plummeted into what they called their little paradise. They'd been having sex for a while, but they'd both been holding back. Or Hazel certainly knew that she'd been holding back and that now she wasn't doing that. "The bawdy slut who lives within me isn't shy anymore," she told Forrest after her first really bone-rattling orgasm had nearly tumbled both of them out of his bed. Her grunts and hollers shocked and amused her.

Maybe her now-riled-up pelvic region had been covertly practicing opera arias just in case Hazel ever stopped holding back and gave it an opportunity to express itself. Forrest, too, had changed but compared to her unequivocal excitement of body and voice, the difference in him was subtle. Actually, she thought, he'd even become kind of feminine. Whereas he'd been considerate of her before, he'd also taken the lead in moving them toward orgasm.

Therefore—and there'd be a certain point when she knew this was going to happen—she'd sense him moving out ahead of her, abandoning the project of bringing her along. She hadn't resented it, she'd just figured that was the way the male apparatus worked. Her choices were to fake an orgasm, to try to persuade herself that she'd had a minor one, or just to pout in her disappointment over missing out on the one truly sublime experience available to living creatures.

From her teenage years, one of Hazel's deep fears was that she would be a failure at sex. Men would want nothing to do with her because she wasn't sexual enough. Forrest's going ahead without her had brought up that old anxiety. She knew he intended no criticism, but she couldn't help taking it that way. What he intended was to move the train of his libido down the tracks and into the station. She'd had enough experience with orgasms to understand that.

Hazel thought Forrest must have consciously decided to stop taking the lead at a certain point in their sex, but she wasn't certain. And she didn't want to bring it up with him, because then she'd have to confess she'd been frustrated. Also, she wasn't clear about exactly how he was different now. Maybe he was confident she was likely to have an orgasm if he just waited for the signals she couldn't help giving—now that she wasn't holding back.

They didn't talk about sex and what they liked and didn't like, the way Doctor Ruth advised her listeners to do. Hazel thought of their recent accord as their bodies having worked it out between them. Words would have made their sex an intellectual project. Grunts, sighs, and hollers did the trick. Hazel was grateful to Forrest for figuring her out. She was tempted to tell him the phrase she'd invented—"Forrest screws well with others."

She thought anyone who claimed to have achieved complete sexual liberty had to be lying. Especially if that person said it happened because one morning she and her lover had about ninety seconds of deeply seeing each other. She wasn't about to announce her good fortune to anyone she knew. She had few friends anyway and none with whom she wanted to discuss Forrest and herself and their orgasms. She realized now she'd never talked about sex with anyone.

She worried that she and Forrest might be just making it up. Maybe they were both deluded. Maybe they'd just gone a little crazy together. "People do that, you know," she told him one evening. Forrest said no, it was real, but the big change was in her. In their first weeks together, he figured she was keeping him on probation, and now she'd granted him the status being her official lover. "I don't know why, but all of a sudden you've let me be your man."

"With all rights and privileges," she said, pulling up her pajama shirt and flashing him. He grinned and reached for her. She trusted his desire for her to be as strong as hers was for him. Again and again there was that balance. He particularly liked looking her over. "We're playing doctor, yes?" she asked him once in bed when he was sitting on her backside and probing her shoulder blades. "I'm just looking for evidence of wings here," he murmured to her.

Forrest was capable of studying her body for hours at a time. She luxuriated in lying still, letting him do as he wished. He pressed and probed. Even her scalp. And maybe especially her feet. "Your toes are just so intricate!" he exclaimed. They were lying side by side in opposite directions, and she was half-drowsing in the pleasure of his investigating the bones in her feet. She wondered if she should enjoy someone playing with her feet.

She was aware that she wasn't nearly as interested in his body as he was in hers. But she decided that was probably just a standard male-female difference. Then she realized that although his intense physical attention pleased her, it hadn't made her take any more interest in her body than she'd ever had. His certifying her as physically desirable enabled her to just forget about it. *He likes what I've got so I don't have to worry about that anymore.*

A ridiculous idea that came to her was that she'd be delighted if Forrest ever said something like *This is an excellent body you have here, Hazel.* Or even *These are splendid boobs!* Of course he was not likely to do that. And what they had—intimacy, sex, lively companionship—was better than any fantasy she'd ever allowed herself to entertain. "We're the astronauts of 872 West End Avenue," she told him one morning. "The two of us alone in space."

Their hermetic state had to change when the new semester began. Their different programs gave them schedules that denied them the time together they'd gotten used to having during the long Christmas break. The West End was a kind of space station for them. They'd meet there for drinks and usually make their way back to the apartment to cook and eat dinner together. They liked walking down Broadway, bumping hips, tipsy from the drinks they'd just consumed.

But of course their friends—most of whom were Forrest's—

would beg them to go with them to Forlini's or the Japanese restaurant down Broadway a few blocks. Their friends sometimes got along, but more often they turned their noses up at each other and said dreadful things about the ones in the other group. "I think they're playing tug of war with us," she told Forrest. "And you and I are ropes?" he said. Even so, these were easy days and lighthearted conversations.

Their pleasure and affection in each other seemed permanent to Hazel. She and Forrest agreed that their solidarity wasn't ordinary. They knew no couples who were as tightly and happily bound as they were. Hazel couldn't account for her good luck. When she considered her life before Forrest and the magical morning, she thought she must have been a seriously troubled person. "I had a lot of anger in me," she told him. "No idea where it came from," she said.

Forrest listened when she tried to explain to him how gnarled up in herself she'd felt. How everywhere she looked she saw people manipulating other people, behaving stupidly, mistreating folks who already lived with constant and overwhelming misfortune. "All I could see was money—and the people who had it—ruining the planet and each other. Everything I saw was hateful. I just ingested it. Maybe that was my defense. Becoming a hateful person."

Forrest told her he couldn't imagine her as a hateful person, she hadn't seemed that way to him even that first time they talked in the West End. She told him she was glad he hadn't picked up on it. They were quiet for a moment. It felt like their first conversation had happened a long time ago. "Not hateful," Forrest murmured, stepping close and putting his arm around her. Hazel was moved both by his words and by the semi-hug that went with them.

In that comforting moment she also understood something she knew she would keep to herself. Forrest couldn't imagine her being as spiritually disabled as she was, because he had never been even close to such a state of misery himself. He was an incorrigibly sunny fellow. But like her, he was who he was. And probably he had to be that way to lead her out of her personally inflicted shadowland. How could she be anything other than grateful to him for that?

Even so, wasn't his sunniness a kind of limitation? *Leave that alone*, she advised herself. *Don't go there.* But her brain couldn't leave the question alone. The answer was obvious: whether or not his sunniness was a limitation, it worked for her. *If there's a problem here, it's all mine*, she told herself. *There is nothing wrong with him. There is nothing wrong with us.* She'd constructed a problem all by herself. Now she had to work through it all by herself.

Toward the end of March the city underwent a sudden change in the weather. In a single day the Upper West Side went from dreary winter to full-on spring. Though the temperature was only in the mid-fifties, it felt balmy. In the sunlight people slipped out of their jackets and coats. As she walked to her Literacy & Society class Hazel noted how many silly smiles she saw on the faces of pedestrians on Upper Broadway. She knew she was wearing one herself.

That afternoon the West End was so exuberant the bartender put on Irish music and some customers started doing jigs in spite of how crowded it was. When Hazel walked in, she wondered if she'd be able to stay. Even on a day like this, she had a limit to how much frivolity she could tolerate. Once inside she looked for Forrest, though she didn't see him until she moved deeper into the fray. But then there he was toward the back—dancing with someone.

Nothing wrong with dancing, she murmured into the massive roar of music and shouting. She stood still a moment to process the cause of the disturbance that rose in her at the sight of Forrest's body bobbing and swaying. *He's even doing dance gestures with his hands*, she noted. Surely it wasn't jealousy she felt—she couldn't even see his dancing partner. It was that he'd never danced with her. He'd never mentioned that he could dance or that he liked it. She stood still in the crowd long enough to be bumped a couple of times by people moving past her. To watch her lover like this—with his having no awareness of it—struck her as wrong, but of course it wasn't her fault. If he looked in her direction, he'd see her, and she'd probably wave at him. But something was working on her that made watching him illicit. She was spying on him. She actually stood up on tiptoe to try to see who he was dancing with.

Well, she did see. Forrest was dancing with two women. She didn't recognize them, but she'd have bet a lot of money they were undergraduates. Probably Barnard students. Nothing suggested that they had any special interest in Forrest or that he was hitting on either one of them. They all three had that aura of dancers caught up in the music and themselves. They were dancers enjoying the trance of their bodies moving under the influence of music.

She had read a novel once in which a wife coming home caught sight of her husband through a side window and inadvertently witnessed him picking his nose. Hazel distrusted her memory, but in her mind what the wife saw turned her stomach and destroyed the marriage. At the time she'd read it, she'd felt some pity for the husband. Who doesn't pick his nose when he thinks he's completely alone? But she'd also felt involuntarily sympathetic to the wife.

Forrest's eyelids were half shut, and he was sweating. His mouth shaped the words of the song—it was Martha & the Vandellas' "Dancing in the Streets." Hazel could tell he wasn't really singing aloud. He'd confessed to her that even though he adored music, he was slightly tone-deaf and incapable of singing on key. And so this was what he did—she'd seen it more than a few times, his mouthing the words but keeping his voice too low for anyone to hear him.

When the song ended, Forrest and his partners had a group

hug. The girls slapped him on the back and fanned themselves. A few people clapped. If Hazel had had a camera, she'd have taken pictures of the three of them in their post-dance giddiness. But she felt horrible! On the one hand she empathized with Forrest's obvious pleasure, but on the other hand she could not stifle her sense of having been cheated out of joy that should have been hers.

He still hadn't seen her, and she didn't want him to until she'd calmed herself. She kept her eyes on him while she moved away. This, too, was an act that she recognized as dishonoring their relationship—she definitely would not use the word *love* even though that word had been hovering over them for many weeks. *I am doing the wrong thing*, she told herself. But instantly she mounted her defense—*If he is who he is, how could he object to my being the way I am?*

She thought she'd managed to slip back into the crowd, but she hadn't yet figured out what she was going to do once she was out of his line of sight. Order a drink, she supposed. She knew she didn't want to walk down Broadway by herself. That would be so sad she'd probably get weepy and have everybody giving her sympathetic looks. She felt a hand on her shoulder and turned to find a shiny-faced Forrest smiling at her. "Where you headed?" he asked.

He pulled her into his arms and held her tightly. She let it happen so as not to have to speak right away. This was exactly what he did whenever they met in the West End—take her into his arms and hug her with conviction, which never failed to persuade her that he truly cared for her. "I've been dancing," he said, releasing her from his embrace and looking into her face. "God, did I enjoy that!" Words didn't come to her. "Are you all right?" he asked.

So he'd seen trouble in her face. But if she could find the right words and the right tone of voice and answer fast enough, they'd glide right into their usual late-afternoon pleasantness. She willed it to be so. Or she willed herself to speak. "I'm fine," she said, dispatching what she hoped was a smile to her mouth. In this moment of his still lightly holding onto her arms and searching her face, Hazel felt herself about to burst with self-loathing. His tightened lips told her that he knew she wasn't all right. "Do you think we can find a place to sit down?" she asked, nodding her head toward the line of booths against the far wall. She knew she was on the verge of losing control, and she really didn't want to say or do anything stupid. She decided her only choice was to try to explain herself to Forrest. Which might very well make him see that she wasn't fit for any halfway-normal relationship.

Better that he see the monster she was than to lie about her feelings or just to let the relationship implode because she lacked the courage to reveal the whole truth of herself to him. "Back there," Forrest said, pointing toward the dimly lit back corner of the West End. It was actually an area of the bar where couples sometimes went to express physical affection in a semi-private setting. An insider joke was that babies had been conceived back there.

Hazel and Forrest both knew what people were thinking as they made their way back to the corner booth, but she didn't care. She figured his willingness to go there meant that he understood they were about to have a serious conversation. As she followed him, she wondered why neither of them thought to suggest going back to his apartment to have their talk. It was a strange choice and one they were making together without a word of discussion.

A question she had entertained from whatever age it was that she became aware of having her own thoughts was whether everybody had a private self they kept out of sight or only a few people were that way. It had always mildly troubled her. Her own hidden self was like a twin who was so beastlike and despicable in human terms she couldn't allow anyone to see it. Which was odd because her social self was rather fond of her feral self. She respected it.

They sat opposite each other. She felt Forrest waiting for her to speak, but she didn't want to look directly at him, and she needed a little time before she started talking. She wasn't even sure she could do what she had in mind. After all, here she was twenty-seven years old, and she'd never revealed her beasty self to anybody. The booth gave her some encouragement—it was set off from the bar enough to feel private, even sort of cozy. And it was dimly lit.

I can do this, Hazel told herself. She sat up straight and turned to face him. As if she'd already confessed something dreadful to him, she felt one of those lightning surges of embarrassment circulate up through her body. He looked grim, as if he were already judging her. His face was that cubist mask she'd almost forgotten about since the morning she saw him reading in the sunlight. But then it did its trick of revealing its owner's generous heart.

"You haven't murdered anyone, have you?" he asked so softly she almost didn't hear him. "No," she replied with a tight smile. Then she began telling him: "But I've wanted to kill more than a few. I've actually felt the gun in my hands, pointing it, and pulling the trigger. Sometimes a pistol, sometimes a shotgun or an automatic rifle. Mostly I shoot them in the face, but a few I've hated so much I've pumped bullets into them even after I knew they were dead."

His expression stopped her. She thought he'd probably look that way if he'd actually witnessed her doing the killing. "You know about guns?" he asked. Even his voice was tinged with horror. "Not really," she said. "But my dad took me target shooting a few times. And I've shot rabbits and squirrels." He blinked and kept quiet. She could see him struggling with his feelings. This was how she'd expected it might go. She had an inkling of how it might end, too.

But now that they were into it, she was certain she could tell him everything. Truth was, she was excited. She knew a lot she was going to tell him, but she also knew there was more, things she'd forgotten, maybe things she couldn't know until she tried putting them into words. She'd be thrilled if she found out something about herself she didn't already know. She was sick and tired of all she knew. She sat still and studied Forrest's changing face "What about the people you shoot? Who are they?" he asked quietly. "My mother, my father, my brothers," she said. "My Aunt Sophie. Jack Gardner from kindergarten. Professor Corey, my statistics professor. Ronald Reagan. That guy who worked for Nixon—Gordon Liddy." Forrest sat back in the booth and gazed at her. "Should I go on?" she asked. His face was neutral, but she thought she detected interest. *He wonders where this is going. Well, I do, too,* she thought.

"Sometimes thinking of a particular person I just want to kill him. Or her. Politicians. People on TV. But others I have to think about. My parents and brothers. I feel guilty and evil for having imagined shooting them. Not so much with Aunt Sophie. After she died I didn't want to kill her anymore." She felt herself flashing Forrest a wry grin. Why not? Her heartless sense of humor was part of the picture. Didn't she want him to see it all?

"Sometimes it's just a thirty-second mind-clip. Like a quick and mean exercise. But I've also had extended daydreams of tying men up and sexually mutilating them. Strangers I've seen on the subway or construction workers who've made their comments to me when I walked past them. And I've seen myself spitting in women's faces. Women who struck me as too pretty, too self-satisfied or nice." Now she saw that she'd gotten to him.

Forrest looked as if he might stand up, walk out, go back to his apartment, and throw all of her belongings out on the sidewalk. And wasn't this what she wanted? She leaned forward. "I thought about doing that to those two little sluts you were dancing with." She sat back and leveled her eyes at him. There was still so much more she could tell him—a catalogue of appalling daydreams she'd constructed, willed into being even if just to savor in her own mind.

If he asked for more, she had it available to give him, but she knew he wouldn't make the request. She was pretty sure he saw the complete picture. The peculiar thing about what she'd just told him was that it was only partially true. It was like a translation of what she knew about the rotten mess inside her. The parts about her family were accurate. But she'd made up the thought of spitting in women's faces. Her brain often invented scenarios like that.

Forrest turned his eyes away. "Those girls were dancing with each other," he murmured. "One of them bumped me and made me spill my beer. She apologized, and then they both asked me to join them. Insisted that I dance with them. I did—you saw that—and I'm glad I did." He stared at his hands. Hazel knew it was time for her to shut up. He sighed. "It was like dancing with my cousins at a wedding," he said softly, more to himself than to her.

He stirred himself, sat up straight and gazed around the bar. She saw his emotions working on him. He was starting to feel the need to get away from her. Nothing good could come from sitting in this booth and letting her throw more of her excrement in his face. In a moment he'd probably stand up and leave her sitting here by herself. She wondered what words he'd find to tell her goodbye. He turned his face to hers. "But I'm sorry it hurt your feelings to see it."

Then he raised his voice. "I'd take that part of it back if I could." Suddenly he leaned forward and took her hands. Which shocked her as if he were shooting jolts of electricity into her. Shocked her so much she didn't think to pull away, she just let him strengthen his grip on her. "You do realize that I love you, don't you?!" His voice was hoarse, and his face was so close to hers she couldn't help receiving the truth he'd spoken. The God-awful truth.

TEN

Turns out that my Aunt Hazel had a couple of old black and white pictures stashed away in the bottom drawer of her bedroom dresser. She explained to me that they weren't candid snapshots, because cameras back in the day were unwieldy, and the film they used was expensive. So the pictures were almost always posed even though they might have been taken at parties or family celebrations. She said there were at least two she would show me, but she wanted us to look at them one at a time. The first one she brought down from upstairs was of her and her mother.

I can't say that I was ready for this encounter with an image of my Grandmother Watson. Which I guess is appropriate, because evidently my grandmother was not ready for the button to be pressed on the camera. She's dressed up for this picture, but her face reveals a pain of such intensity the viewer can't help wondering what the cause can be—stomach cramps, a headache, a sprained ankle? Then it quickly becomes clear. My grandmother—who must have been in her late thirties when this was taken—has her eyes fixed on her daughter. And my Aunt Hazel's face shows that she hasn't a clue of how her mother is regarding her.

She's ten, wearing a dark-colored dress with a white collar. Her face might be considered plain were it not for what I'd have to call an intrepid intelligence. If I were to write a caption for Aunt Hazel in this moment, it would be something like *I know I have to go to this stupid birthday party, and I don't expect to have a good time, but I will survive it because I'm smarter than any of the other kids who will be there.* Can a ten-year-old girl arch her brow ironically? Well, maybe not, but some seventy years into the future that's what her face in this photo tells me.

And she probably is aware of what her mother is thinking in this moment. Which I'd say is approximately *What kind of life is my child going to have when she's not pretty, she has a sharp tongue, and she has no interest in people her own age?* The irony here may be entirely in my mind, because I've come to know my Aunt Hazel well enough to understand that in spite of her adamant inclination to be alone whenever possible, she's had a rewarding life. She knows I admire her, when almost no one else in the family does. And especially now, as we're sitting here with this picture that shows what she was up against with a mother who views her with a pained expression. "My mother suffered a lot of disappointment in her life," Aunt Hazel tells me quietly while we look at the photograph. "I knew I was the cause of some of it, but I felt sorry for her."

Checkers

When Aunt Hazel brought down the photograph of her father and herself, she didn't hand it to me immediately. I was sitting at her kitchen table, but she didn't just take a seat and hand it over. So I asked her why she didn't want me to see that picture. "I don't know what I'll say about it, John Robert." Then she handed it to me, but she still didn't sit down. From the picture itself, I couldn't see what the problem was, so I must have looked up and raised my eyebrows. "Well, I know," she said. "We're just playing checkers, and we're not looking at the camera.

"My mother must have been the person who took this. If she were alive, she'd probably have a lot to tell you about my father. He was an inarticulate person. My theory about him—which I probably thought up when I was five or six years old and have held onto ever since—was that his feelings were so intense that he tried to protect himself by saying as little possible. It wasn't a problem with my brothers because with them he could play catch or toss the football around or shoot baskets in the driveway. And he could talk sports with them. But what was he going to do with a daughter? And what was a daughter going to do with a father who couldn't talk to her?

"He finally answered that question by getting out his old box of checkers and the board that went with it and asking me if I wanted to learn to play. Of course I said I did. I couldn't have been more than seven or eight then, and his invitation touched a place in me that had been aching for quite a while. I wanted his attention. Young as I was, I'd nevertheless had thousands of hours of observing him, and I'd learned so much that I didn't even realize I was taking in. For instance, he didn't enjoy my mother's company, but he pretended that he did. My brothers often made him angry but he forced himself not to let them see that.

"I think his secret was that he was a deeply fearful man, especially about the members of his family. He thought my brothers would hurt themselves with their reckless playing—which of course they did, though Walt's broken arm was the only serious injury. He didn't trust my mother's driving, he didn't like to be in the car when she was behind the wheel, and he was almost certain she'd wreck the car if he wasn't along to advise her. I knew he worried about me, maybe more than he did the others, but to this day I have no idea what harm he thought was coming to me. The worst I could imagine was that I'd get hit by a car or have a bicycle accident. But I was a careful child. I was often on the verge of telling him that he needn't worry about me."

HOW IT ENDED

1970 — New York City, Upper West Side

❧

IF HAZEL'S NOT EXACTLY HAPPY, IT'S NOT HER FAMILY'S FAULT. Her Methodist parents said a blessing at dinnertime, and they attended church mostly because they liked the hymns.

Her brothers teased her until she yelled at them, but they never embarrassed her at school or in public. She wishes they'd talked to her, but maybe they didn't know how.

And maybe it was odd how her parents insisted that their private space and that of each of their children was to be respected. In Hazel's family, if you were in a room by yourself with the door closed, you were not to be bothered.

The privacy principle gave Hazel a chance to read, pay attention to her thoughts, daydream, or make things up. At the time she never thought this remarkable, but as a grown-up she knows it was the part of her childhood she most cherishes. But yes, maybe it made her too much of a loner.

Could you blame your parents for allowing you to develop the most necessary part of yourself? From the age of thirteen Hazel had felt the need to get away from people. All right, she can't deny that she's intolerant of others.

Also her social skills are not the best. She doesn't know what to say around people who chat to pass the time of day or who try to replicate dialogue from situation comedies.

Her brothers and her father monopolized the one TV in their house to watch sports. Thus Hazel equates TV with boredom. The way she was raised allowed her to become who she is.

⁊

She can't think about Forrest without blushing with shame. No finer person ever lived. To get free of him, she had to convince him she'd go on hurting him until he let her go.

It was mostly that she was trapped in her perverse ways, but Hazel blames the apartment for some of what went wrong. To be specific, she blames their tiny bathroom and kitchen.

Apartment 2B of 872 West End Avenue had a huge living room-dining room and a decent-sized bedroom with a large closet. It had high ceilings, an exposed brick wall, and a bay window that faced the street and let in plenty of light.

That big room was an elegant space. It was nicer than any of their friends' apartments. Hazel was a graduate student at Columbia, and Forrest worked for Simon & Schuster on 43rd Street. She thinks maybe Forrest had talked her into moving in with him, but the apartment closed the deal.

Its little rooms worked on her in cunning ways. Forrest liked to cook, and he also liked Hazel's company in their kitchen. She bumped his elbow at the stove, and he burned his hand. He spilled soup on her favorite sweater.

They joked that they lacked the footwork to cook together. But Hazel was slow to forgive him for ruining her sweater—even though she knew he didn't blame her for his hurt hand.

She wished she could get rid of her ridiculous grudge-holding inclination, which made her feel like a werewolf.

Forgiveness wasn't something Forrest had to think about.

⁊

Hazel thinks she could write a novel called *The Bathroom*.

The first time Forrest walked in on Hazel while she was peeing, she shocked both of them with the fit she threw.

When she'd calmed down enough for him to speak, he said, "Haven't we taken showers together? Don't we have sex?" She left the apartment and slammed the door behind her.

She walked down to 57TH Street before she turned around. When she entered the apartment, she told him she didn't want to talk about it, and he obliged her. They both slept badly that night, but when she woke all her anger was gone.

Over toast and coffee they chatted as if nothing had happened. This was a new dynamic for Hazel. She'd never been so angry. And then to have the upheaval between her and Forrest just dissolve? It was like a rattlesnake had appeared in their living room and then disappeared.

And the rattlesnake was hers. She hated her shrill voice shouting those ugly words. She hated being that monster and wanted never to behave like that again. Especially since what had set her off really was such a small thing.

But she also had to admit she didn't want Forrest walking in on her again when she was peeing. It probably wouldn't happen. But other bathroom behavior had begun to annoy her.

He often didn't clean the toilet after he'd used it and left streaks for her to see. And he left stink in there.

Also his careless peeing meant wet spots around the toilet.

℘

That little bathroom forced Hazel to see her small soul.

Unfortunately she couldn't keep herself from keeping track of the tiny offenses Forrest committed in the bathroom.

Hazel wasn't shy or squeamish, but she couldn't make herself talk to Forrest about it. The conversation might have hurt his feelings, but he'd have been fine about it.

She did manage to tell him that he should clean his hairbrush occasionally, that she was frustrated when he tried to talk with her while he was brushing his teeth, and that he should cut his toenails more often than he did.

But Hazel wasn't good about putting away clothes, shoes, books, or papers. She didn't like washing dishes. Yet her ways didn't trouble Forrest. He picked up after her. When he found dirty dishes in the sink, he'd just wash them. He did these things cheerfully. She felt guilty all the time.

On weekends Hazel usually had reading to do and papers to write, while Forrest never brought his work home with him. So he vacuumed, shopped, and took their dirty clothes to the laundromat. Then took her out to dinner and a movie.

Hazel knew the problem was all in her mind. Forrest wasn't keeping track, but she couldn't make herself stop noticing every little task he did and everything she left undone.

Nor could she just make herself pick up her clothes and wash the dishes when it was her turn, which would have been easy.

But evidently she needed to be both victim and perpetrator.

∓

One sunny Sunday morning they decided to take a walk.

It was mid-May, the winter had been long, then it rained all through April. Forrest said they needed some sunlight.

Truth was, Hazel was tired of her grumpy, critical self, and she was determined to stop being such a bitch. In the soft air she felt like she was coming back from the dead.

Forrest was telling her how their blocks of West End Avenue were sort of like a small town. Hazel wasn't saying much. The sun on her face made her feel lazy and slightly aroused. She placed her hand lightly on Forrest's triceps.

Hazel felt her dreamy mind struggling with what she saw

half a block ahead of them—a young man pulling at a woman's purse. He kicked the woman, she fell down, and Forrest started running up that way, shouting, "Stop that!" The young man ran with the purse, and Forrest chased him.

Hazel began running, too, her head clearing as she ran. She needed to tell Forrest to stop chasing, he could get shot. The young man dodged traffic to cross the street. He turned down 108TH Street with Forrest close behind him.

It took so long to reach the corner that when she did, she saw Forrest coming out of a building, carrying the woman's purse. Then he smiled at her, and Hazel started sobbing.

Forrest kept his arm around her as they walked back to the woman being comforted by people who'd seen what happened.

The woman kissed Forrest's hand. "My hero!" she told him.

∽

What the woman did and said made Forrest blush bright pink.

Hazel kept seeing Forrest chasing the young man up West End Avenue. Certainly a hero. But hadn't he also been a fool?

When they went out to dinner that night Forrest told her what happened in the building. He said the purse-snatcher was no older than fourteen and evidently had no weapon.

"The kid saw he'd trapped himself in the foyer. He was scared and sweating. He threw the purse at me and ran out the door. Getting the lady's purse back was all I cared about. I was going to try to talk him into giving it up."

In the soft light of Forlini's, Forrest's face captivated Hazel—she'd forgotten how smitten she'd been with him when she first glimpsed this startling beauty he had that was visible only in certain settings. *How can I not just completely love this man?* She made herself stop gawking.

Later, waiting for him in their bed, Hazel watched Forrest

undressing and told her mind to shut up about how foolish he'd been to chase that boy. He turned out the light and came to her. *Every man should be such a fool,* she thought.

The next morning Hazel felt like she'd forgiven him for something. After he left for work, she walked all around the apartment, stopping in the kitchen and the bathroom.

She knew her mean thoughts and ungenerous soul couldn't be the apartment's fault. But the idea kept pestering her.

In all of these rooms Forrest's looks were unexceptional.

જ

Simon & Schuster fired everybody in Textbook Editorial.

Forrest had known that "a purge was coming," as he put it, but he hadn't thought he'd be among those let go.

Hazel had believed him months ago when he told her he was the only person on his floor who kept regular hours, often ate lunch at his desk, and actually produced textbooks.

He'd told her about editors who came to work late, took three-hour lunches, then dropped by the office on their way home to ask their secretaries if there'd been any calls. He'd said his boss liked him and appreciated his hard work.

When he came home and showed her the termination letter, he cried. The only thing Hazel knew to do was to put her arms around him and murmur such comforting words as she could make herself say aloud. Forrest drank three stiff gin and tonics and went into the bedroom at 8:30 and shut the door.

Their living room sofa was also a fold-out bed, so she had a place to sleep, but she was shaken by this fallen version of Forrest. He'd never been even slightly inconsiderate to her. Hazel wondered if she'd have it in her to help him.

"I have to go on welfare" were the first words he said when he came out of the bedroom. He stood by the fold-out bed, staring at her. "Oh bubsy," she tried. It made him wince.

She'd heard a classmate say that to a friend who was ill. But Forrest had heard how phony it sounded on her tongue. He left early to get in line at Unemployment Benefits.

༄

Forrest found out freelance copyeditors were in demand. Since the going rate was fifty dollars an hour, he could stay home and make a couple of thousand dollars a week.

His even temperament came back almost as quickly as it had disappeared. "Money doesn't exactly make me happy," he told Hazel, "but lack of money sure does make me unhappy."

He'd never been fired before, never been without a job. "If I'd known I had a talent for this kind of editing, I'd have quit office work a long time ago. My old high school English teacher made me the best copyeditor in New York."

Forrest inhabited the apartment all day every day. Hazel had classes and meetings and library work to take care of up at Columbia, and he usually had dinner waiting for her when she came to the apartment. She considered telling him it was her frequent hugs that had gotten him back on track.

It was late summer. Their days and nights were enjoyable. Evidently Forrest's repairing himself had fixed Hazel as well. She could overlook or navigate the little things about him that had turned her into such a harridan before.

But the dissenting voice within her had not been completely purged. It emitted little snorts and whispers. *Don't forget how weak he was. Or how you had no respect for him.*

When his parents came to visit, she and Forrest slept on the sofa bed so that his parents could have the bedroom.

After their goodbye hug, Forrest's mother beamed at Hazel.

༄

She tried imagining weddings she might be able to tolerate.

She'd vaguely thought when she finished at Columbia she and Forrest would say goodbye and promise to stay in touch.

She accused herself of having a high school mentality, but that didn't help her to take a positive view of a long-term relationship with Forrest. Or with anybody she'd ever met.

"I know this is going to hurt your feelings," she told him one morning as she was leaving to go to class, "but I just realized I'm not a monogamous person. I don't see us going on and on." When he looked up at her, she closed the door.

She was ashamed of herself. Her face felt hot all the way up to campus, and she kept telling herself that it was a kindness to let him know where she stood. But she knew that what she'd said was cruel, and saying it on the way out was cowardly. She couldn't stop replaying the scene.

All day she felt her jaw tightening with what she recognized as her belligerent mode. Wrong in her thinking, callous in her behavior, she wouldn't apologize or take it back. Her mantra became *He'll be better off without me.*

In her Ed Psych class, they'd had a unit on adolescent issues of esteem. She knew what the common wisdom was—her words and actions showed she had a low opinion of herself.

But her problem was the opposite. She cared too much about the rest of her life to hand it over to Forrest Garrison.

"Are we ever going to talk?" he asked when she came home.

&

Exit phase—surely he understood that's what they were in.

They were passing through a very peculiar phase. Hazel was on her best behavior. Forrest wasn't trying to please her.

So far as she could tell, he had no animosity toward her. If he still loved her, he was keeping it out of sight. She thought maybe she had a kind of emotional allergy to love.

In December, when her coursework was finished, they'd agreed she'd move out before the first of January. Rather than "the break-up," they called it "the parting," both of them careful to enunciate the phrase with cheerful irony. Hazel had found a job working for the State of Vermont.

"You know what, Forrest?" He was shaving, and Hazel had just turned off the shower—they'd actually gotten so they could share the bathroom and could even enjoy chatting with each other in there. "I think you should get a dog!"

She took his silence to mean that he was thinking about her idea. When she pulled back the shower curtain to reach for a towel, she saw that his whole upper body had turned red.

Forrest shaved in the nude, and the fury of his face made her forget the towel. They were two feet from each other.

Then he went back to shaving, and she closed the curtain.

First Grade

"You see this little girl right behind me and to the left, the one with the bangs and the braids and the gap-toothed smile? That's Lucy Beth Groseclose. She and I had these ecstatic times of playing together at recess. That was where I learned everything I know about complete joy. Lucy Beth didn't teach me, she was just a person who knew how to get there. And I doubt she knew what she was doing or that the fun we had was anything special. I don't know if it's a curse or a blessing that it can be that way for one person with another—you're about to faint with the gladness of connecting soul to soul with somebody, while that person is just passing the time of day.

"As I recall, Lucy Beth and I were engaged in the construction of a leaf palace for a katydid shell we'd found. And there was something about our four hands scrabbling around in the leaves and grass and dirt under this huge willow beside the playground. Our construction site, I suppose I should call it. What made it magical was the way the breeze sifted through the leaves over our heads and the way the sunlight and shadows skittered all around us and washed over our hands while we were building the leaf palace. We used twigs and sticks and rocks to make a kind of structure, but of course it was all so precarious that the structure kept collapsing or small pieces would blow away.

"Once I even caught Lucy Beth, either accidentally or deliberately, knocking over a little formation—the Queen's dressing room—that I'd managed to put together. Maybe that was the real pleasure for that girl—knocking over parts of the palace that I'd very carefully constructed. It's been seventy years since I last saw Lucy Beth, and I suppose it's silly of me now to suspect her of having a destroyer impulse. I didn't see it then. What I did see was a sweet-faced girl who made me laugh with her odd facial expressions and the silly goatish noises she made.

"There might have been some bath soap fragrance around her, a scent I've never again smelled on anybody, and it could have been sunlight and the air temperature that released that scent into the air—all of that probably went into the shimmering ecstasy I experienced and thought I was sharing with Lucy Beth. I also suspect her—nowadays—of having no such experience herself. No matter. Lucy Beth was the love of my life. And the only reason I can say aloud such a worn-out phrase is that it tells the whole sad sweet story of what I did. Loved another kid because she was fun to play with for a few spring days in first grade."

Easter Girl

This one was taken before they all got in the car to go to the Easter service. Hazel looks to be around twelve, though she could be younger. She's standing between her brothers, my father and my Uncle Walt. The boys have on jackets that are too little for them—my dad said their parents didn't even try to keep up with buying clothes that fit them because they grew too fast. My granddad probably tied their ties for them, because Easter was just about the only time those boys wore ties. The brothers have great smiles on their faces, probably because they'd been horsing around and putting on a show for the neighbor who took the picture.

My grandparents stand behind the three kids, and they're both smiling in a way that makes them look very American and very proud of their kids. When I showed this picture to Aunt Hazel, she said it was the first time she'd ever taken a good look at her parents' faces in it, and the fact that they looked so happy surprised her. "I'll tell you the reason for those smiles, John Robert—they were so pleased to have us all dressed up in our Easter clothes and out of the house and ready to get in the car for the drive to church.

"Those mornings of getting ready to go to church were just wild, with my brothers cutting up and teasing me and our mother trying to look just right for the ladies of the church and our father not all that happy about going to church in the first place. They're smiling because they've survived the chaos that went on in the house. From this point on, they know it's all going to be easy. But to have gotten all three of us out of our beds, into our clothes, and out of the house and lined up to have our picture taken—for our parents that had to be like winning a major battle."

Aunt Hazel kept studying the picture with this rapt expression on her face. I could tell she was reliving that morning. So I asked her the question I wasn't sure I would have the nerve to ask her. "Why do you have such a sour look on your face?" She looks like the Queen of Pouting. She's wearing a white pleated blouse buttoned all the way up to her neck and this very pretty long skirt that must have been pink, and her hair was brushed and shining in the sun—but she herself looks like she's got a burning hatred of everybody within ten feet of her. I told her, "You look like you're just about to turn one way and slap my dad, then turn the other way and slap Uncle Tommy." She laughed and laughed about that. "You're right, I look like I'm about to hurt somebody," she said. "But it was just my braces. They hurt my gums and really made me uncomfortable."

THE ARRIVAL OF JOHN ROBERT

1980 — Burlington, Vermont / Hanover, New Hampshire

తు

A BOY HAD BEEN HAZEL'S SECOND CHOICE, BUT WHEN TOMMY phones to tell her he's here, tells her his name, and says he's almost ten pounds, he has dark hair and a set of lungs like Pavarotti's, and he wants to meet his Aunt Hazel, she says she'll be there as soon as she can get there. In this most villainous winter since Ethan Allen nearly froze to death on his horse-drawn sled crossing Lake Champlain, Ms. Hicks drives through a blizzard across the state to get to Dartmouth-Hitchcock Hospital to see John Robert in his first day of breathing oxygen. Hour-and-a-half drive takes her four hours.

About this boy she'd expected to be of two minds—in fact that's how she'd have preferred it, because of course she has no children of her own, she's just turned 41, and she has little to no interest in babies in general. Also the baby's father, her brother Tommy, though she supposes she's obligated to love him, has inflicted little-sister teasing and torture on her for so many years and at such a high level she thinks she can have him put behind bars if she ever wants to press charges. But when Tommy says the child's name, the sound of it pleases her ear, and she thinks maybe finally there's somebody in the world she can adore without complication.

On the Newborn Nursery floor, Hazel heads straight to the

viewing window to look at the babies. She's been hoping John Robert will be easy to identify—she thinks it important to establish rapport between a boy and his aunt without the interference of parental spin and static—but there are seven or eight little human units in there all in a row, swaddled up and capped so that they look like recruits in a baby army. A couple of them are squalling, four have their eyes closed, but one of them is open-eyed and calm, so that's the one Hazel studies. When a nurse comes out, Hazel asks her which one is the Hicks baby, and the young lady points to little Mr. Open Eyes. Hazel stands there shivering with the pleasure of having correctly identified her new nephew.

When she walks down the hall to the Hicks room, Hazel finds Tommy looking like Jesus has just tapped him on the shoulder. Yesterday describing the face of her brother would have probably been an easy assignment—hardcore Republican set of the jaw, pirate blue eyes, hair trimmed so close it's almost a shaved head, and a mouth that's designed for bad-mouthing welfare cheaters and talking trash in sports conversations. Hazel's brothers have always been found hard to take by relatives, parents, teachers, coaches, human resources officers giving presentations on diversity and sexual harassment, and even by each other. Whenever she's around her brothers for any length of time, Hazel wishes she was anybody but a Hicks.

This afternoon, however, Tommy has a sweet docility about him that bemuses Hazel. "Hey, brother, you look like a human being today. What's wrong?" Tommy just smiles, wraps her in a big hug, and pats her on the back as he has never done before in their whole lives up until now. Tommy's wife, Teresa, the mother of John Robert the Open-Eyed, who is ordinarily extremely put-together and by-the-numbers cordial to Hazel, sits up in bed with storm-tossed hair and none of her usual makeup, looking like she's ready to declare war on anybody who even says hello to her. Hazel stays an arm's length away from that bed and avoids eye contact with its occupant.

Hazel gets the picture. Her brother has wanted this baby probably since not long after the wedding, and Teresa has been ambivalent almost as long—she has a fast-track job at People's United Bank, and she knows that birthing this kid is going to set her career back at least a couple of years if not permanently. Plus there is the matter of the ten pounds of John Robert that has resided in her belly for nine months and a week and that must have been no fun at all when it made its exit around 3 A.M. As someone who recognizes a negative family dynamic when she sees one, Hazel thinks she, too, ought to be making an exit pretty darn soon.

The problem is that she wants to hold that boy in her arms, wants it really badly. This particularly stupid yearning is not familiar to her—she thinks it's utterly at odds with her character, and yet here it is refusing to let her start moving toward the door, making her excuses, acting like she can hardly wait to get back out there on the Interstate so she can drive the four hours through the blizzard back to Burlington. When she notices a chair over in the far corner by the window, Hazel makes for it, thinking that if she just keeps quiet (which is a skill she has) and doesn't get in anybody's way, she can stay there incognito until the nurse brings in John Robert, and then maybe she can think of some way to ask if they'll let her hold him. Or maybe Tommy, in his new saintly self, will ask her if she wants to.

The boy's mother looks like she may refuse the baby when they bring him to her. *Not mine,* she'll say, *that thing doesn't belong to me,* and she'll raise her hands, palms out to fend off the bundled-up lump of newborn creature they're trying to shove into her arms, and that's when Hazel will stand up and say ever so calmly, *Here, Teresa, I'll take the boy and just sit over here and hold him awhile until you get used to him.* Ah, Hazel—she's still got her wishful kid fantasy powers fully intact; she sometimes thinks she could have had a very rewarding career as comic book heroine, *Hazel in the Wings* it would be called, about a woman whose life kept taking detours without ever reaching any destination whatsoever but who steadfastly continued to believe that there was something mysterious and fantastic waiting just for her out in the future. When the smiling nurse does bring John Robert Hicks into the room, Teresa raises her arms toward him and instantly transforms herself into a woman whose only desire from birth to this moment has been to nurse this baby.

Still Hazel keeps sitting quietly in her corner thinking maybe it can happen; as long as she's here in the room there's a chance that boy will find his way into her arms. The misery she feels here is, in a general way, utterly familiar to her—she has this overwhelming desire for something that's so close she can see it in detail but that's out of her reach unless somebody (over whom she has little influence and no power) decides to be generous and give her a little taste of it. *A tiny spoonful of righteous pleasure*, she thinks, that's all she wants, and she can't just ask for it because she knows the answer will be *No, not now and no forever more, you want it too much; therefore, the answer must be, So sorry but not in your lifetime.* "Hazel, do you mind holding this baby a minute while Tommy helps me to the bathroom?" Teresa asks, and suddenly she's smiling like they've been best friends ever since high school.

So the instant before the baby's body moves through space into her arms, Hazel's brain undergoes a whirly-gig spasm of pleasure. As her transmogrified brother carefully deposits the startling weight of the boy into her hands then steps back to steady his wife on her three-step journey to the bathroom, Hazel's concentration shuts out everything in creation except the tidy, blanket-wrapped package of this most extraordinary nephew. She can feel the heat of him in her palms. Probably it's against the rules, but Hazel nudges the cap off his head—"The better to see the tippy-top of your noggin, dear boy," she chortles softly, meanwhile marveling at how sappy she's gone under the influence of human replication as it manifests itself here before her eyes in the form of blood kin—*Lord God!* she thinks, *he smells like he just came out of a cave.* She smoothes her palm over his warm scalp and whispers, "Welcome to the most impossible family on the planet, kiddo."

A random kindness bestowed by the universe folds time around Hazel and her nephew. In real time, as the NASA folks might say, Hazel probably has no more than eight minutes of holding John Robert, gazing at him as if she can read his future in the puckery smacking of his lips and his dark eyes that appear to be studying her face, blinking only occasionally. She makes a little chant out of his name and sings it to him, she loosens his swaddling enough to gain access to his hand, she opens his fingers and gently places her fingertip in his palm, she puts her nose right up to his forehead and inhales deeply, and when the child yawns she holds him up to her face so she can peer over his tongue and down into the red tunnel of his goozle. Tommy's hands appear before her—he's there to transport John Robert back into Teresa's arms—so Hazel lifts the boy up and over to Tommy with little reluctance, because it feels as if she's spent a year with that baby. "I think he's hungry," she murmurs.

Then Hazel sits in her corner, ignored by everyone else in the room and softly resonating as if she's just splashed down at the end of a long journey from outer space. A little lightheaded, she tries to grasp the muted drama playing itself out in front of her, though it's hard for her to follow what Tommy and Teresa and the lactation specialist are talking about—they seem so far away, and it's as if she's a ghost among living people. Hazel understands that she's just experienced an ecstatic encounter that she must have yearned for all her life, something that evidently has disassembled her interior life sufficiently that although she feels at peace with everything around her, she also has no sense of connection to anybody in the room except John Robert. Like deepening twilight, a gradual sense of not existing at all descends upon her.

Whatever this is that's come over her is not unpleasant. She considers standing up and stretching, shaking it off like sleepiness or a bad mood, but she isn't ready to give up the pure freedom she feels—these lovely competent adults in the room are absorbed in the project of John Robert's having his first first meal on this side of the womb, and they've so completely forgotten she's here that she might as well not be. The words *not be* suddenly and lightly touch some previously untouched circuit of her brain, so that she witnesses a rapid sequence of images, a little video her mind plays for her: Tommy turning toward her chair, not seeing her and asking where Hazel went; Teresa not taking her eyes off her nursing son and saying, "Oh maybe she went to the bathroom, or maybe she was tired and just decided to drive back to Burlington"; the lactation specialist glancing from Teresa to Tommy and wondering who they're talking about, never having noticed her in the first place; and strangest of all, the empty chair, this chair warmly occupied by her body this very moment, suddenly empty of her. Hazel knows she's in an exotic state of mind, one that makes it clear to her that now that she's had her time with John Robert, her presence in this room is necessary to no one—it's a presence that might as well be an absence. So she stands, quietly gathers up her coat and bag, moves to the door, and opens it. "Goodbye, everyone," she says softly, blowing a kiss (something she's never done before) to her nephew. As she eases the door closed behind her, she hears Tommy and Teresa calling, "Goodbye, Hazel."

She wonders how long this state of mind or spirit intends to have its way with her. Down the elevator and through the labyrinth of fluorescent-lit hallways and into the gloomy parking lots, she somehow remembers her way back to her car, all the while enjoying her contemplation of that baby boy in her hands, warming and brightening her thoughts. Ordinarily the prospect of driving at night through bad weather would have her mood in a chokehold of despair, but paying her parking fee, finding her way out of Hanover, making her way to Interstate 89, she's as cheerful as a bank robber who knows he's never going to be caught for the heist he's just pulled off. Because her nephew is so tangibly present in her thoughts, her eyes, her hands, and even her lap, she's kidnapped him. In her mind Hazel has John Robert Hicks right here with her in the car, resting on her lap with the crown of his head against her belly and his legs extending under the steering wheel as she drives.

The Interstate still has long patches of ice, but at least the snow has stopped falling, the stars have appeared in the sky, and there's very little traffic. Around Woodstock her treasuring of John Robert gradually transports her into remembering her Aunt Wilma Ransom, the old maid who came to live the last weeks of her life with Hazel's family. Hazel knows it's a mental association that could occur naturally only during a late-night drive on an icy interstate after many hours without rest and an intense first encounter with a newborn nephew to whom she has responded with her whole heart. And it must be the physical intimacy that is the connection—in the old lady's dying Hazel bonded with her Aunt Wilma so deeply that at the very end, she climbed into bed with Wilma and held her bony body through the last breaths she took. If she could have, Hazel would have accompanied her Aunt Wilma right on into death.

Hazel knows she's damned peculiar for the way she thinks and feels. Right now she thinks that evolution must have placed her on the planet as an alternative version of human, that she's lucky the authentic humans haven't locked her up somewhere, and that she still has her freedom, probably because most of the time she's been sly enough to keep her thoughts to herself. Okay, so however irrational and odd she is, she's not going to resist whatever revelation it is that's gradually moving into her consciousness as she drives this solitary highway toward her house in Burlington. Yes, now she's beginning to see how she's had only a very few physical connections with other human beings—this one with her nephew who's not yet a day old, the one she had with her lover Forrest Garrison, which lasted about seven months, and the one she had for a few weeks when she was thirteen and held her Aunt Wilma in the last hours of her life. There were two others, but she refuses to think about them right now. "Just these three," she murmurs softly.

Three's enough is the thought that comes to her, and the one that follows is *I wouldn't have wanted more than three.* She's wide awake, she's had the car on cruise control for long enough that it feels like the machine almost doesn't need her, she just has to move the steering wheel every now and then. Something about her headlights tunneling through the darkness pleases her mightily. She suspects she's still so high from her encounter with John Robert that everything is feeding into her serenity, her sense that all will be well, and that during this long day and night the universe must have decided to set her free of obligation and the special variety of suffering that has been her lot as an alt human. Now that her magical nephew has arrived, her life will be a continuation of this skimming smoothly through the night, following the lighted path always before her, moving on and on toward no destination whatsoever. Then she sees that this must have been how it was for Aunt Wilma in her last days—the old lady understood that the destination didn't matter and nothing was required of her. The path of light was taking her where she needed to go.

Hazel knows her brain to be both foolish and relentless in its workings. Ordinarily she would berate herself for submitting to such wispy musings, and what she thinks of as her iron will would step into the discussion and insist that the hard facts be taken into account: Hazel has no real friends; Tommy and Teresa don't enjoy her company, and so there is no reason why they would wish her to have any influence on their son; Hazel treated Forrest Garrison so brutally in breaking up with him that even if he didn't hate her then, he most likely despises her now; and the reason Aunt Wilma Ransom asked Hazel's family to take her in was that she, like Hazel, had no friends, and now that she's dead, Hazel is probably the only person on the planet who remembers her even slightly. Hazel carries out this review of the hard facts while her car glides past the Richmond exit. In another fifteen minutes she'll be home, and she's astonished that her state of mind has not been shaken by all the bad news she'd dredged up to be taken into account. Even the obvious conclusion—that there is no path of light—doesn't strike her as anything she has to take seriously.

There's no baby on my lap either, she murmurs, *but as long as I feel him here, here is where he is.* She smacks her right thigh three times with her non-steering right hand as she takes Exit 14w and steers the car around the long curve and up onto Williston Road toward the university. *My mind may be peculiar and flawed as a failed invention, but it doesn't depend on being right about anything, and it is strong like you wouldn't believe.* She's passing the Sheraton on her right and the Staples Mall on her left, and still her car feels airborne as a spacecraft to her—the machine just goes where it's supposed to, with her mind and body tending it only slightly. *No path of light necessary,* she murmurs as she crests the hill and coasts down past the university buildings. She turns right on Prospect Street, and she's pulling into her driveway and switching off her headlights when she's blinded by a vision of such power and vividness she has to blink and squint and feel for her keys with her hands in order to shut off the car.

Hazel's body has landed pushed forward on her side so that her head, arms, and torso lie on her wooden kitchen floor while her derriere, legs, and feet lie on slate tiles of her foyer. She looks like a fallen runner. It's shadowy in here, the foyer light's on, but the kitchen is lit only by the light over the stove that she always leaves on. Her gloves are off but she still has on her coat. One of her boots lies on its side near the door, the other's still on her foot, so she was probably stricken just as she was struggling to get her damn blizzard boots off. From her seat in the dark in the car, Hazel can feel the blow of the thing hitting her like a kick to her solar plexus, can feel herself toppling over. She moves in close to get a look at her face. The one eye she can see is mostly closed, but her mouth is open as if she's saying something, or maybe it's just a grunt or an "Oh!" Hazel can't imagine what she might have said as she fell, though she knows it must have been a shock to realize that she was taking a tumble. In spite of Vermont's icy winters, she hasn't fallen since she was kid. *So this is how it is*, she thinks, viewing the scene from the car—and maybe that was the dead woman's last thought. *So this is how it is.* The car has gotten so cold that the engine's not even ticking anymore, and still Hazel can't free herself from what she's seeing. She can't, in fact, get loose from her state of being both dead in her house and alive here in the front seat of her car. This is not so much a thought as it is a whole-body realization that comes to her here in the dark. *I feel so sorry,* are the words that follow the emotion.

I feel so sorry for anyone who has to find this body here in my house. She considers who the finder might be, fireman, police-man, or rescue squad EMT—in any case a stranger. She bows her head. A gentle sorrow pushes her to cry a little, but Hazel is not about to allow herself any sobbing or tears. Though she's in no hurry to let it go, the vision's gradually loosening its hold on her. *Something good here,* she thinks, and she strains to grasp what it might be. She's aware that this entire journey across Vermont has been so surreal she might as well have been on drugs. "I've been on ecstasy!" she snorts to the car that's now so cold she's starting to shiver. She opens the door, stiffly climbs out, stands in her driveway stretching, bending backward with her hands on hips, gazing up at the starry sky. "Do you remember me? Look at me down here! Hazel Hicks! Am I not healthy as a horse?" she demands. She strides to the side door of her house, unlocks it, latches it behind her, switches on lights, removes her coat and boots, shakes the building with her deliberately heavy steps in a circle around her kitchen table. She taps two fingers on it, and whispers, "See? I told you I wasn't dead." And when she finally goes upstairs and puts on her nightgown and slips under the covers of her bed, Hazel whispers, "Night, night, John Robert. Sleep tight."

First Chair, Second Trumpet: Part iii

Aunt Hazel asked me to come back for tea again the next morning, and when I arrived I could tell she'd been waiting for me. She started talking while she poured my cup of tea. "John Robert, I've been thinking about some of the boys in that band—Maynard Kegley, Henry Crabtree, Kent Umberger, Tommy and Bobby Potts, Ronnie Ireson. They were athletes and farm boys and half-hoodlums who didn't care about school and slept through their classes and got into fights during lunchtime.

"It wasn't like the band made them different people—they were who they were, but during band practice and when we were playing concerts and football games or marching in parades, those boys were like professionals. They'd try to help other kids who might be having trouble with the music or the marching maneuvers or even just the stamina to march five or six miles in the summer heat. Henry Crabtree and Maynard Kegley carried those huge bass drums, flailing away at them, and the Potts brothers carried Sousaphones, swinging them while they played, and those guys sweated through their whole uniforms when we had to make those long marches.

"But what I've just been remembering is how much pride they took in playing the music. Ronnie Ireson was famous in school for being a clown in social studies and for Mrs. Parsons sending him to the principal's office every other day. But he played snare drum in marching band and tympani in the concert band, and he had so much talent that everybody including Mr. White was in awe of him. When Ronnie was in the band, he possessed dignity; in just about any other aspect of his life, he was a screw-up. I'm telling you this because it was those boys, finally, who broke the news to me—that it was probably not my destiny to become a great trumpet player.

"I had let it slip that I wanted to go to the same college Mr. White had attended and to become a band director like him. I hadn't really intended for anybody to know my dreamy little plan, but somehow Sue Kilby got it out of me, and even though I made her swear she'd never tell anybody else, she did indeed tell."

Aunt Hazel sighed and made this soft stuttering sound that I realized was her trying to laugh at her teenage self. But I knew something wasn't right with her. When I glanced at her face, I saw she was blushing and was on the verge of crying. So I looked at my watch and started yammering about having to be somewhere in ten minutes. When I asked her if I could come back tomorrow to hear the rest of the story, she nodded.

First Chair, Second Trumpet: Part iv

The next morning, while she was pouring our tea, Aunt Hazel picked up where she'd left off. Her voice sounded very determined. "It was Henry Crabtree—who'd always been nice to me— who took it upon himself to tell me that I probably wasn't going get to be what Mousey Spence was in his senior year, First Chair, First Trumpet. 'You're good, Hazel,' Henry told me. 'You're a strong player, you work hard, you care about what you're doing. But the way you're good is Second-Trumpet good. I'm telling you so you won't break your little heart wanting that First Chair. Wanting what Mousey's got. That's not going to happen for you.'

"Of course I asked Henry how he could know my future, but he just shook his head. He might have heard Mr. White talking about me, but I don't think so. I think Henry had talked it over with the Potts brothers and those boys in the percussion section. I think they got together and discussed all the serious kids in the band and decided among themselves just how good we were and how far up we could go in our sections. In spite of how much his words hurt my feelings, Henry was very kind in the way he spoke to me. He thought he was doing me a favor.

"And you know what? Henry actually patted my hand and gave me a little hug around my shoulder after he finished delivering the bad news. After he broke my little fifteen-year-old heart." Aunt Hazel stopped there. She wasn't exactly looking me in the eye, but I could see that she was proud of herself for having told the story all the way through to the end. I could also see that some of the pain of it was still with her. "You're sure he was right?" I asked as softly as I could. She sighed again and bowed her head and didn't say anything for so long that I thought she just wasn't going to answer me at all.

Then she did speak, but in such a low voice that I leaned

toward her. "I'm not sure, John Robert," she said. "I believed Henry. And now I can't ever know. I just stopped trying so hard and caring so much. I would stay First Chair, Second Trumpet, until I graduated. At the end of my junior year, Mr. White talked to me and explained how important it was to have a strong player heading up that second section and how much he appreciated my effort and my ability. He said I was good enough to be in the First Trumpet section but he really needed me right where I was. So I accepted it. That's who I became—the person you see sitting here: First Chair, Second Trumpet." She stood up, put her hand on my shoulder as she walked by me, and went upstairs.

PRONE

1982 — Burlington, Vermont

❧

PRONE TO A MILDLY PARANOID VIEW OF THE UNIVERSE AND HER place in it, Ms. Hicks figures the weather is out to teach her a lesson. She can't imagine what she's supposed to learn, but she thinks it probably has to do with her daily harvest of hope and despair. Heavy on the despair side.

Ms. Hicks has diagnosed herself as everyday bipolar. A sunny morning with the city's crabapple trees dropping blossoms on the sidewalk stupefies her with spiritual yearning. Sleet slapping her face from a February wind makes her wish somebody would shoot heroin into her veins.

She has learned weather has its own code of conduct and most likely won't kill her or even make her crazy enough to kill herself. *Don't like the weather? Just wait a few minutes.* Ms. Hicks thinks the local folk say this as a mantra against their uneasiness with ever-changing weather.

A lesson from the weather could be okay. Depending on the content. She doesn't like the way she is—how she thinks, feels, or behaves. Problem is, even if she could change, there are no good role models. Male or female. Just lots of lousy ones. At least she can say *I'm glad I'm not so-and-so.*

A man stands on a street corner asking pretty women who walk by him, "Wanna fuck?" He gets dirty looks; he gets kicked, slapped, punched, kneed in the balls. Somebody asks him, "Why do you do this? You're taking a hell of a beating." The man says, "Yes, but I get a lot of fucks."

Ms. Hicks thinks that joke is almost the story of her life. *I'm taking a beating because I really want something. It's not exactly a fuck, but I think it's similar. I'm okay with the beating, it's just that I'd like to get a little of whatever it is that I want. I wish I could say what it is.*

Ms. Hicks has her house and her badly tended flower garden out back. She knows she's done little to deserve these benefits. She won't say *blessings*—she's purged that word from her vocabulary. If she were homeless she'd kill herself as dramatically as possible. Set herself on fire.

The roof over her head is her defense against everything. When big storms rampage through her city at night, Ms. Hicks wakes up and feels her house shaking. Sometimes she goes out to her garden and squints up at the sky. *Go away*, she whispers. Take your nastiness off of my property.

Fact is, she respects weather. Especially lightning. Only an idiot wouldn't take lightning seriously. Thunder makes dogs tremble. Cats run under the bed. Ms. Hicks thinks even elephants must get nervous when they see lightning. Giraffes are probably the most afraid of all. Poor dears.

Ms. Hicks put in a crop of begonias. Dug up dirt to make shallow holes, added store-bought manure, gingerly removed the young plants from their plastic cartons, gently placed them roots down, lightly packed dirt around them. Got her hands dirty. Did her best to savor the dirt fragrance.

No children but I've got my garden. No husband but I've got weather. Weather's faithful. It lies to me, but it stays by my side wherever I go. Flatters me in April. Takes me to the beach in August. Then in February it kicks me around the house and tells me I'm an ugly old hag.

She entertains herself. Like eating her croissant topless.

Warms it up while she's still half asleep, goes to the bathroom, pulls off her nightgown and dines in front of the mirror. *Nice boobs,* Ms. Hicks tells her mirror self. *Don't talk with your mouth full,* her mirror self tells her.

When she first went to college and read D. H. Lawrence she took to walking in thunderstorms. That must have been when she and weather started up their bad romance. She'd come back into her dormitory soaking wet, shivering, teeth chattering. Maybe she was daring the lightning to hit her.

Maybe lightning would have struck her if she'd been pretty, but she was plain then and more so now. She had a few months of prettiness as a sophomore in high school. Like her physical self was trying to make up its mind which way to go. She wasn't pretty long enough to get her hopes up.

Plain is better. Plain girls develop stronger inner resources. Ms. Hicks thinks maybe she overdid it. Her own thoughts seem so much more intriguing and funny than those of anyone she knows. Whenever she tries to lower her standards and socialize, people give her funny looks.

Being plain doesn't bother her. What rankles her is wanting something desperately without being able to figure out what it is. Not Jesus. Not even full-time ecstasy. She spends a lot of time staring out her window. The birds that come to her garden won't put up with her pouty ways.

Birds persuade her that science is a whimsical genius. And that maybe when the weather does teach her a lesson, it'll be kind to her. It's not kind to the birds, but if they're unhappy it doesn't show. When she sees a junco or a chickadee riding a gusty wind she wishes she could do that.

She's eating lunch by her bird-watching window when she sees a scruffy man just walk into her backyard. She can't see her gate, but he must have unlatched it. His dark jacket and pants have that shaggy, long-unwashed look of the homeless. But he's focused on something back there.

He's wearing a baseball cap pulled low on his forehead, so she can't see his face, but she sees that his scraggly hair has long needed cutting. He's taking slow steps as if he's trying to sneak up on something. Well of course, now she sees it! A little wing flapping over in the back corner.

You can't just walk into somebody's garden, she'll tell him. She leaves her sandwich on its plate and fetches her warm sweater from the closet. It's April and not yet warm. When she steps out her back door, she feels her heartbeat. The man must be drunk or crazy, but she's not afraid.

She's not so much angry as she is curious about why somebody would trespass so openly. And why *her* backyard? Ms. Hicks's house looks respectable, but it's small and ordinary. It's a house that makes a statement. *Not much money here,* it says. *Who lives here isn't worth robbing.*

"Hey!" she says. Staccato but not quite a shout. Startles herself more than she does him. He's right there, maybe ten yards away. Without turning to face her he uses one hand to make a palms-down gesture in her direction. He's no taller than she is but shapeless in his lumpy clothes.

She can't tell if he's skinny or fat. The thought occurs to her that this person could be woman. She squints and looks carefully and decides it's a man. A darned nervy fellow to shush her and not even look at her. But at least he's not threatening. She looks where he's looking.

It's a house finch having a sort of seizure. She's never seen a bird act like this. She's also never seen anybody so interested in a bird they'd trespass on private property to watch one die. Yes, it's a pretty thing, reddish head and neck, grey striped breast, but finches are common.

Ms. Hicks sees no need to sentimentalize the death of such a creature. There are probably three or four house finches hatched for every one that dies. What's their life-span anyway? A couple of years? This is a part of herself she doesn't admire. She's fairly sure she has a stunted soul.

To get a better look at the dying finch, she steps toward it. Which short journey takes her almost alongside the homeless man. *My intruder,* she thinks. *My intruder could use a bath.* The bird flops onto its back and twitches. Ms. Hicks thinks it's obviously in its final moments.

The man takes three strides, bends, and scoops up the creature. He stands and gingerly works at clasping its wings to its body. He seems unaware of Ms. Hicks. She's barely aware of herself. With both hands he holds the finch so that its head pokes out between his forefingers.

The bird blinks, but it also looks calm, maybe even comfortable in the trap of the man's hands. It makes no sound. *Maybe the little thing thinks it's dead and this is how it goes in bird afterlife. A giant comes along, picks you up and holds you carefully in its warm palms.*

This is one of the ten thousand silly thoughts that visit Ms. Hicks all the time. She knows she's smarter than most people, but she also knows her mind can be that of an unruly five-year-old. She's noticing that her intruder's hands are big but not clean. Then her eyes meet his eyes.

His face is pie-shaped, oddly pink, and bigger than she expected. His eyes, nose, and mouth are too small for such a face. He looks like a character in a children's book. His expression is mindlessly sweet and alert but also suspicious. He squints at her. He's damaged, she thinks.

Evidently he has sized her up and decided he doesn't need to account for himself or what he's doing. He glances around, taking in her weedy little garden, the back of her house with its peeling paint. Also her windows are filthy. Who is he to be making judgments about her and how she lives?

He heads for her rag-tag lawn furniture, a metal table and two battered metal-and-wood beach chairs—pieces on the sidewalk with "Free" signs on them she found on her walks. No one but her ever sits out here. Holding the finch with both hands her intruder plops himself down with a grunt.

She's followed him to her makeshift patio arrangement. Now that he's sitting down she expects he'll speak. She stands and waits. He says nothing, doesn't look at her. He's a rag pile. She's five feet away, near enough to take in his garbagy smell. He studies the bird like it's a book.

"My house," she says, lifting her arm in what she intends to be the gesture of a person who's made something of herself. She considers making another gesture toward his dilapidated shoes and saying, "My land." The rag pile doesn't quite shrug, but she knows he's thinking about it.

Now Ms. Hicks glances around her garden, her house, her neighborhood. It's not much of a place. Her parents scrimped and saved to pay off the mortgage and leave it to her. She's made no improvements. She can barely pay the taxes. She knows the neighbors sneer at it and her.

The rag pile begins whistling softly and tunelessly. He's looking at the finch, but surely he's not whistling for the bird's benefit. Ms. Hicks sits down in the other chair. Her intruder has taken the one she usually sits in, and she hopes this one won't collapse under her. She watches him.

It's mid-April, a fickle time of year in Vermont, but this afternoon the sun feels pleasant to her. The rag pile is not what she'd consider human company, but she finds herself relaxing as if he were an old college friend who's come to visit. She's never known a homeless person.

Because she lives by herself, with her imagination serving as something like a companion, Ms. Hicks isn't surprised when she falls into a peculiar spell. She envisions taking on the rag pile as a project. Cleaning him up, sharing her food with him, coaxing him into communicating with her.

Ms. Hicks is also long accustomed to entertaining ridiculous notions, and as she studies her intruder—who seems to be wearing at least five layers of clothing—she recognizes the thought of taking him in as ranking among her all-time worst ideas. *I'd kill him or he'd kill me.*

She sees his eyes flick up toward her face, and she could swear the corners of his mouth twitch into about a five-second grin. He lifts his hands with the bird in them up and slightly toward Ms. Hicks as if he's offering it to her. She sits up straight and prepares to receive it. *Does he really mean to give it to her? Is she really going to accept it?* The rag pile ever so slowly opens his hands. The bird fluffs its wings slightly but remains sitting in the rag pile's two palms as if nesting. It blinks, then stands up on its legs that are like twigs with tiny talons.

Ms. Hicks is enthralled by the sight of the finch swiveling its head like a beautiful toy. She's never been this close to one. There's a sudden soft *pft!* as the bird streaks off and away. In an instant it's gone. Ms. Hicks is both exhilarated and bereft. Her intruder watches her intently.

She's a little stunned by the intimate presence of the finch followed quickly by its absence—as if an exquisite painting she'd begun examining had been whisked out of her sight. Also the strangeness of her intruder and his behavior feel like a dream from which she can't wake up.

Ms. Hicks remembers a sixth-grade classmate, a loud and obstreperous boy, whose nickname among the children was "Big Face." She gives her head little shake and instructs herself to focus. She realizes she's defenseless and not a very competent person. She's has zero survival instincts.

The two of them are watching each other now, but she thinks they aren't really exchanging looks as people do who want to communicate. They are two animals, each estimating its chances of overcoming the other. She remembers a saying of her mother's: *It's so easy to be nice to people.*

She never thought her mother had much common sense,

but she's about to ask her intruder if he'd like something to eat when he stands up and shakes himself. *Like a dog or a horse*, Ms. Hicks thinks. Then the man actually smiles at her. *He's beaming*, she thinks. *He's beaming down on me.*

He pats her shoulder as he steps past her. Then he's out the gate and gone. *He's very good at exits*, she thinks. The unappealing smell of him lingers around her, but she's not ready to move. Her feelings are in an uproar. At the moment they are mostly a mix of sadness and well-being.

And that's what I've been wanting? she asks herself. It's the well-being part of it she means. The sadness is to be expected. In fact she expects it to expand and bully the other feeling until it goes away. *I'm too easy*, she thinks. *All I need is a smile and a pat on the shoulder.*

The sun keeps her warm, and she hears bird song, though the birds keep themselves out of sight. She thinks that's as it should be. After all, the look she just had at that finch may last her for the rest of her days. Finally, though, the air turns chilly. She shivers and stands up.

☙

Mornings now, Ms. Hicks awakes and rises from bed without her daily measure of fury. Her days don't entirely lack occasions for bad temper. When she reads or hears the news, she's quickly riled up as usual. If a car drives too fast down her street, she shakes her fist at it and shouts.

But now her rages dissolve. Her bad temper has no stamina. Even the loneliness and sorrow that used to keep her simmering seem to have lost their hold on her. She thinks her new self lacks backbone. *I've been upgraded*, she says aloud with a little snort. *Against my will*, she says.

She accuses herself of being a fool for missing her old unhappiness. She'd be embarrassed if anyone knew how she'd savored being so irascible. *Maybe I was just putting on a show*, she thinks. But that's not true. She doesn't like admitting it, but she knows she felt hurt all the time.

Afternoons she goes out to her garden. She actually does a little work out there. Mostly just weeding, but one day she gets down on her knees and puts in whole row of pansies alongside the fence. *Big pansy plants a bunch of little pansies*, she mutters. She hasn't lost her sense of irony.

The thing with feathers is screwing up my life becomes her mantra. She knows the intruder won't be back, she just wishes she could purge him from her thoughts. She gets weepy when she brings up the evidence of his taking an interest. *Didn't he pat my back?!* she demands of science.

Next thing you know I'll be going to Sunday School, she tells science. *Their big guy couldn't possibly pay less attention to me than you do*, she says. More and more it pains her to glance out her window and see the empty beach chairs where they sat. The sight of them is the rag pile's insult.

So she's almost back to her former self when—wouldn't you know it?!—she glances back that way and there he is. Not just sitting but leaning back in the chair with his hands clasped at his belly, his hat off, his face turned to the sun. He hasn't changed his clothes since she last saw him.

Ms. Hicks's first thought is *What an odd-shaped head he has!* Her second thought is to call the police. She's still got the salt in her for such meanness. Her third thought is one that's familiar and hateful. *What if I'm hallucinating? What if the cops come and think I'm nuts?*

She steps closer to the window. If he evaporates in front of her eyes, she'll know for sure she's nuts. He's still as a statue. Or a cadaver. The mild stink of him comes back to her, though of course she can't really smell him from where she stands. She can't imagine why he came back.

He's no threat, she tells herself. If he were knocking on her door she might have a reason to be worried. She goes to the kitchen to fetch an apple, then tiptoes back to the window. She is foolishly pleased to see him still sitting there. She goes back to the kitchen for a knife.

This is not exactly a plan she's thought through, but she feels as if she's acting decisively. From the kitchen she takes her paring knife, the apple, and a saucer. She exits the back door, walks at a normal pace out to her makeshift patio, and sits down in the chair opposite her intruder. She hasn't looked directly at him yet. She's not sure why. She sets the dish in her lap and cuts the apple in half. Now she does look at him. He's sitting up straight, scrutinizing her. *He's completely ready to leave*, she thinks. "Would you like half of this apple?" she asks him.

Ms. Hicks has kept her voice neutral and her face pleasant. The situation interests her anthropologically. Voice, tone, facial expression—those signals must have determined the life or death of many a person. The rag pile doesn't move, doesn't stop watching her. *He could just disappear!*

Ms. Hicks lowers her eyes to the knife, the dish, and the halves of the apple. "I know people who eat every bit of an apple," she says quietly. "Even the core and the seeds. If you'd like me to leave the peel on it, let me know. I've gotten used to peeling each slice before I eat it."

She prides herself on her ability to peel an apple slice quickly, precisely, and with a certain grace. No living person could care about such a skill. Even so, she's aware that her fingers are performing for her intruder. The peeling drops onto the plate. She hands him the slice.

Their eyes meet in the split second of the chunk of apple passing from her fingers to his. She peels a second slice for herself. She's surprised to see him waiting for her. If it's manners, she appreciates it. For some moments they observe each other as they chew their bites of apple.

When she peels another slice, he accepts it. While they finish up the apple, Ms. Hicks decides that the human face is so unappealing in the act of chewing that it's odd they've studied each other's faces while they eat. She's sure that people at dinner parties don't behave similarly.

She sets the plate with the knife and the apple scraps on the tottery table beside her. After some silence, during which they both cast their eyes around the yard, Ms. Hicks folds her hands in her lap and says, "I've been wondering what was wrong with that finch you brought back to life."

The rag pile smacks the fingers of one hand against the palm of the other. The smack is loud enough to startle Ms. Hicks. What interests her is that the smacking hand drops through a foot or so of space with its fingers wriggling slightly. *How the bird fell*, she thinks.

"A car?" she asks. He makes no gesture, though he looks straight at her, and his face tells her she's right. Exactly how his face conveys this she can't say. He didn't move his eyes or mouth, didn't blink, didn't nod. It's as close to mental telepathy as she's ever experienced.

Nothing comes to her to say or do. Her intruder leans back in his chair and lets his eyelids droop. Ms. Hicks feels a little drowsy herself. She's amused to think they're about to take a nap together. Her thoughts meander as they often do when she's alone. She wonders if he can talk.

Something makes her suspect that he can talk but that he's choosing not to. *Maybe he was someone who used to talk for a living. An actor, a newscaster, a pastor, an academic.* She detects herself making up a romantic past for him. *Maybe he was a protester who got beaten up by the police.*

When she jerks awake, he's gone. She hadn't meant to fall asleep. She can't remember ever having done so like this—outdoors and in the immediate presence of another person. She finds

herself reluctant to move. As if she's holding on to the few m
utes she and her guest spent together.

℘

Ms. Hicks is confident he'll come back. The Pattern of Threes
applies. She thinks that pattern is hard-wired into the human
brain. *It's not religion, it's not fairy tales or myths, it's science,* she
argues against the litigious voice in her that whispers, *You'll never
see him again.*

All right, it's a willed confidence. She doesn't care if it's informed by her powerful desire to know more about her intruder.
She's shameless nowadays, though she has her shame all to herself.
Nobody else knows her guest was here. Only she knows about
the finch. Or the apple slices.

Ms. Hicks has had years of training in solitude, more than
half a lifetime thinking her thoughts and feeling her feelings
without anyone else's input. *All by my lonesome* has come to be
her mantra. *Actually,* she thinks, *it always was my mantra, I've just
now discovered the words for it.*

She knows she's her best self when she's without human
company. The actions and words of others call up the rage that
lies dormant within her. She's especially vulnerable to Tea Party
Republicans. She has a vocabulary for them that can be activated
by even a short quote in the news.

Her guest, however, hovers in her mind as more spirit than
flesh, more creature than human. *Probably because he never said
a single word,* she thinks. The last person to whom she granted
this ethereal status was Lucy Beth Groseclose in first grade, she
of the transcendent pigtails.

Of course no one will ever ask her about Lucy Beth, but if
anyone did, Ms. Hicks thinks she'd weep. The times she'd played
with silent Lucy Beth at recess made her whole body resonate

with happiness. Somehow the gleeful look on Lucy Beth's face made her aware of the wild bliss she felt.

She realizes there must have been other times when she was happy without realizing it. She was not a sad child, maybe moody and quirky but rarely sad. She has no use for that word. But she doesn't like the words *happy* or *happiness* either, especially when spoken aloud. Hates to hear them.

In the last few minutes she spent in her guest's company she felt contented and aligned with the world. She felt a kind of rightness about her life. *But if I'd been happy I wouldn't have fallen asleep,* she tells herself. *Happiness is for children, and even then it has no staying power.*

A word that nags her but that she'd never say aloud is *mindful*. It's a word she associates with extremely self-indulgent people who pay thousands of dollars to talk about themselves to a person who takes notes, sometimes asks questions, but offers neither advice nor opinions.

The ongoing discussion she holds with herself is whether or not she is a mindful person. She knows she constantly monitors her thoughts and feelings. She's so self-aware she sometimes has to remind herself that other people are out there. That the world and time exist without her.

So does that make her mindful? Does that mean she possesses mindfulness, that quality that only gurus and highly spiritually advanced people are said to have? Ms. Hicks doubts it. She sees herself as a self-made spiritual lout. She distrusts all religious thinking. Even her own.

Her intruder's first visit was in mid-April, his second in early August. She's astonished that she has continued to believe the rag pile will return to her garden. She no longer uses the term *backyard* for the land behind her house. She has tended it enough now to call it a garden.

In November she stops weeding and trimming, though she still takes her walking tours at least twice a day. If the weather is decent, she'll sit awhile in her makeshift patio. She does that even after she needs a sweater. Then a jacket. She sits until she starts shivering.

A light snow falls just after Thanksgiving. The days are shorter. *He'll come back*, she tells herself in the morning when she wakes up. And she tries to say it just before she falls sleep. *It's not a prayer!* But she feels like she's pushing against something she's not strong enough to move.

℘

Police are investigating the death of a 52-year-old homeless man found inside a tent off the Burlington bike path near Texaco Beach. At this time there is no evidence of foul play. There is some indication that the death is related to exposure, according to police. A toxicology test and autopsy will be performed, police say. An acquaintance of the man notified police, who arrived on the scene shortly after 6 P.M. Tuesday evening and found the man unresponsive in his tent.

℘

Unresponsive is how Ms. Hicks begins to think of herself in the days following her reading about the unidentified dead homeless man. Her custom has been to fetch the paper from her front steps and to read it in her kitchen as she drinks her juice and waits for her coffee to finishing brewing.

She knows it's him of course. The knowledge is so absolute and problematic it feels like she's had major surgery that isn't healing properly. Distasteful as it is to her even to think it, she needs a way to cope with his never coming back. Knowing so little about him should help, but it doesn't.

She cancels her subscription to the paper, though she has to bring in a week's worth of papers until the cancellation goes into effect. She takes them straight to the recycling bin. Because she knows the dead homeless man will be identified, she doesn't listen to the radio or watch the news on TV.

Ms. Hicks doesn't consider what she's going through as grieving. *I am merely unresponsive* she tells herself. Actually it makes no difference what she calls it, no other human being knows about her visits with her guest when he trespassed on her property and sat with her in her garden.

When her parents died she did not grieve. That's when she realized that *grief* was the name other people gave to what she was going through. A painful period of time from which eventually she would recover. Out of consideration to her parents' friends, Ms. Hicks pretended to be troubled and sad.

Each of her parents, however, had been old and ill for many days. They had vaguely wished for an afterlife, but mostly they just wanted their lives to end. What Ms. Hicks felt about their deaths was exaltation. They were free of their suffering, and she was free of watching them go through it.

So the pain of grieving in her experience was in acting like she felt the opposite of what she actually felt. That was troublesome, but her performances were limited to the hours she had to spend with the real grievers who brought her casseroles and wanted to reminisce about her parents.

Ms. Hicks suspected most of them were putting on an act for her benefit. Even so, she's proud of having done the right thing. She knows her parents would approve and be grateful to her for it. They would know that hiding her true feelings was the way she showed the world they'd raised her properly.

Now in these shortened days of January, February, and March, she senses that her flattened-out spirit is an instinctive alignment with the harsh weather and dark season. There are times when she feels herself about to plummet into despair, but she's not about to give in to weakness and victimhood.

She realizes that *I am unresponsive* is what she says now instead of *He'll come back*. She knows her intruder would understand. She can see his face telling her she's doing the right thing. Telling her without a squint, a twitch of his nose, or a tightening of his lips. Just making her know.

౿

I've always thought March was the meanest month, Robert. I hope you don't mind that name. I've needed something to call you that would restore the dignity my other names for you never acknowledged. I've liked almost every Robert I've known, so that's why I chose it. So, as I say, March has always seemed to have it in for me, and it's been no kinder this year. But this time I've found it illuminating. Maybe it's been trying to get through to me all these years, and I've finally gotten the message.

I woke up very early one morning a few weeks ago and couldn't get back to sleep. The wind was whistling around the house, the thermometer said it was 16 degrees out, and I knew I had to do something. It had rained and snowed and sleeted and then snowed again; the sun seemed to have gone into retirement, and I'd been indoors for I don't know how long. I felt like I'd read everything in the house, there wasn't anything I really wanted to eat or drink, I didn't want to hear what the radio had to say, and I was determined not to turn on the TV.

I felt so desperate it actually made me giggle. 4:30 in the morning, two more hours of darkness, and then another whole day to get through. That was when I thought of you. I was so ashamed of myself for being whiny that I felt my face heat up the way it does when I've done something stupid or wrong or idiotic. But the thought of you cleared my mind, and I knew what I had to do. It was like I'd been wandering in some children's-book, fairy-tale forest, and you came along and just nodded your head toward a path. I was suddenly "filled with purpose," as they say.

I put on long underwear and two pairs of pants, a vest, a parka, a hat, a scarf, gloves, boots, and Yaktrax. All that clothing was ridiculous, too, but at least I was doing something other than walking from one room to the next and feeling sorry for myself. I went out into the snow and wind. It was dark, but of course the streetlights were on. The sidewalks hadn't been plowed, but the street was clear, and there were no cars out. So I walked out into the middle of the street and headed up the hill toward the university. I thought the green up there might be a good place to walk.

I was wrong about that, the wind got stronger the farther up the hill I went. I figured March really had me where it wanted me. It had been saving up this special punishment for me, and I was really going to get it now. But I figured I was as ready for it as I was ever going to be. All those clothes were protecting me except for the skin around my eyes between the scarf over my mouth and my hat and parka hood pulled down to my eyebrows. I had to walk tilted forward, and I had to take baby steps because it was crazy windy, and the street had a coating of ice and packed snow.

The sidewalks into the green were fairly clear, so I took the one that led straight to the fountain at the very center. A blast of wind struck me so hard that I actually staggered and had to catch myself with a hand on the back of one of those benches where people sit to watch the fountain in pretty weather. The thought that I might die did occur to me, but I was so insanely alive right then that it seemed like a trivial idea. I was eight minutes away from my warm house. Can a person really freeze to death when she's fifteen minutes away from a cup of hot tea?

But March got my attention back with a super blast of wind that seemed aimed directly at me. It made me sit down on the bench and hunker down over my knees. My body took the cold and wind more seriously than my mind did. I actually made myself stay where I was, and when the wind let up a bit, I straightened my back and found myself gazing at the waterless fountain. The campus lights focused on it with that eerie kind of purple whiteness that turned the whole green into a nightmare landscape.

The wind was blowing a steady stream of sifting snow over the lip of the fountain. This flowing gray-white condensation rose up in an elegant curl. It formed a perfect arc, which then dissolved into nothing. I kept trying to see the exact point where the something turned into a nothing. It was a vision—or as close to one as I've ever witnessed—and the sight was so compelling that I don't know how long I sat there staring at it. I could have died and not even noticed it. Robert, of course the state of mind I was in made me vulnerable to what I was seeing.

I knew that curl of sifting snow was telling me a truth about life on the planet. Or it was demonstrating a fact that was the opposite of uplifting or beautiful or anything like that. I confess I had you in mind, Robert. You were part of the trance that held me there until I started shivering. When I stood up I knew I'd stopped being unresponsive. *That phase of my life was over. I had also come to terms with the perverse way I've been configured by my genetic makeup and the whole history of my life right up until the wind made me sit down on that bench. I made sense to myself.*

As you know, I can hardly stand the company of other people, and yet—as you can plainly see—I'm someone who needs to talk, someone who needs a particular kind of human contact. I'm not nearly as self-contained as I thought I was. Which is why—now that April has brought us some civilized weather—I'll be here in the garden pretty often. You can count on me, Robert. There's work to be done out here. And there are these chairs just waiting for the two of us. It's very kind of you to visit with me here. I appreciate it. And I'm looking forward to more conversations with you.

Just Hazel

My Aunt Hazel has always had this appearance-neutral place in my thoughts, a girl who wasn't pretty, a woman who wasn't beautiful. But years ago I asked my father for this photo of her when she was in college, and he gave it to me. So I've been able to study it as much as I wanted to. Because she and I have recently been looking at photographs and talking about them, I've come back to this one a number of times. She's standing in front of a lake in bright sunlight, with a breeze catching her hair and blowing it a little to the side. No curls, no makeup, no jewelry. She has on a white sleeveless blouse, tucked into loose-fitting navy-blue Bermuda-length shorts. The expression on her face is friendly enough, and her mouth is open as if she's saying something like, "Are you sure you want to take my picture?"

No matter how many times I come back to this photo she's still not pretty, beautiful, glamorous, or attractive. But at the same time, she's appealing in a way you can't put your finger on. My Uncle Walt once said—and I'm fairly certain he was half mocking her—that she was "a vibrant presence." And that's as close as I can come to naming whatever it is she's got that keeps me interested and summons me to visit this picture of her again and again. It's almost as if she is perpetually refusing the categories of *plain* or *shy* or *low-profile* or *no personality*—at the same time she's sort of defending women who might have been assigned to such categories.

I was fifteen when I asked my father for the photo, and he didn't think twice about handing it over. He didn't ask me why I wanted it, which surprised me—my dad generally took any opportunity he could to tease me. And if he had asked me why I wanted it, I would have had no answer. Or I'd have mumbled something like, "I just want it." But a couple years later, it occurred to me that he didn't ask, because he already knew why I wanted it. Aunt Hazel had doted on me from as far back as I could remember. I wanted the photo because she'd always beamed a great deal of attention my way whenever I was around her. A very raw way to put it would be to say that I'd always been aware that she loved me. That I was special to her. But she also was careful not to heap it all over me. Not to guilt me into hanging out with her when I had other things to do with my time. Last year, when I mentioned her to my dad, he gave me a funny look and said, "Your Aunt Hazel drove through a blizzard to see you on the day you were born, and ever since then you've walked on water as far as she's concerned."

EXCRUCIATION

1984 — Montpelier, Vermont

ℰℐ

1984 WAS THE YEAR OF THE GREAT BUDGET SHORTFALL AND THE shocking number of the teacher layoffs in Vermont. Ms. Hicks's department ordinarily had direct encounters with only a handful of individuals whose cases were "vexed" in any given year. In 1984, however, seventy-three teachers were "let go" by their schools; therefore, Ms. Hicks had to help carry out the interviews that were required by state law.

Ms. Hicks considered herself a vexed case. She disliked conversation in general, deplored professional face-to-face encounters of any kind, and could hardly bear conflicted interviews. Her talents as an administrator were research, writing, and what some state legislators called "creative solutions." She had a history of finding ways to resolve conflicts between teachers' unions and school boards.

Governor Richard Snelling, a Republican back in the time when Republicans were still sensible people, had come to admire Ms. Hicks's writing style. Off the record, he told a *Times Argus* reporter she was the only state employee he'd ever known to make him laugh out loud while reading an annual report. The governor sometimes sent his assistants to ask Ms. Hicks for help writing documents he had to sign.

A diplomat in writing, an oaf in person, was a phrase Ms.

Hicks cooked up for herself that she meant to say aloud sometime in the future, perhaps at her retirement party. Meanwhile, she found herself inept and inadequate in her interviews with the sad, angry, and newly unemployed teachers. Beyond their severance pay, she had nothing to offer them. Listening to them was all she could do.

She'd spoken with ten teachers, and she had two more to go when she encountered Lucretia Taft, a young woman from Maine who'd been terminated after her first year of teaching junior and senior English at Hazen Union School in Hardwick. Ms. Hicks met Ms. Taft in a conference room in the Pavillion building on State Street in Montpelier. The two of them sat cattycorner at a table with ten empty chairs.

"I'm Cretia," Ms. Taft said when they shook hands. "Do you mind if I call you 'Hazel'?" Ms. Hicks said she didn't mind. She supposed she didn't, though it struck her as peculiar for professional women twenty years apart in age to be on a first-name basis within a minute of meeting each other. "I'd looked forward to saying all four syllables of your name," Ms. Hicks said. Cretia cocked her head then grinned.

While they settled themselves at the table, Ms. Hicks noted that Cretia had brought no papers to the occasion. The other teachers had placed documents on the table before them. When Ms. Hicks looked directly into Cretia's face she felt a slight stop in her breathing. Neither *pretty* nor *beautiful* occurred to her—they didn't apply—but Ms. Hicks could think of no single word for beyond-beautiful.

Cretia's hair was red and curly, her skin was that pale pink that always seems to be on the verge of blushing, her lips were full, and her eyes were the blue of early twilight. Her skirt, blouse, and jacket, however, were impeccably modest. Ms. Hicks thought Cretia must constantly have to tone down her appearance to keep people from gawking. Ms. Hicks forced herself to stop staring at the young woman.

Cretia was smiling, not so much at Ms. Hicks but evidently at the room itself. Her demeanor suggested she had come to this interview to accept a job rather than to beg to be allowed to keep the one she had. Ms. Hicks knew that she was twenty-three years old, a graduate of Bates, and the only first-year teacher in the history of Hazen Union School ever to receive a perfect score in her first annual evaluation.

"Have you ever taught?" Ms. Hicks shook her head. In fact when she was a graduate student at Columbia she'd had a semester of student teaching at P.S. 75 Emily Dickinson on West End Avenue. Rather than explain to Cretia that she had been unable to conquer her fear of students sitting at desks eagerly waiting for her to teach them something, she simply denied that she'd once wanted to become a teacher.

"It's really something," Cretia murmured. Now she seemed to have turned her full attention to Ms. Hicks and to be peering into Ms. Hicks's face. "I'm kind of amazed that I survived this past year. I still can't believe how intense it is. 'Was,' I guess I should say. I had kids who were so smart they scared me and others whose souls seemed to have been murdered before they even got to high school."

As she spoke, Cretia's face became animated, though she sat still and seemed unusually calm for someone who'd just lost her job. So far as Ms. Hicks could tell, Cretia was simply making conversation. From her previous interviews she'd come to expect these teachers to make some kind of case for themselves. Ms. Hicks knew they deserved to be heard, but she hoped the discomfort she felt didn't show in her face.

Cretia leaned forward enough to startle Ms. Hicks a little. "Hazel," she said. "I cared for some of those kids so much I thought I must be breaking some kind of law. I worked so hard for them I made myself ill a couple of times. I had to take sick days just to get some rest. The first night of Christmas break, I slept for eighteen hours straight." Now Hazel suspected Cretia wasn't just making conversation.

If Cretia had an agenda that she was working herself up to present, Hazel had a canned statement she would have to recite to her. And Hazel really didn't want to do that. She'd helped draft the statement, but that didn't keep her from hating to read it aloud. *The State of Vermont blah blah blah.* It made her feel like a soldier who'd suddenly realized he was fighting in a war he didn't believe in.

"But you know what?" Cretia went on. "Back at the end of March when the snow started melting and we had some pretty days, I took each of my classes outside for a little walk out to the playing fields and back. I asked them to stick together and behave themselves. I told them it was fine if they talked but please not to make a lot of noise. I hadn't asked Mr. Gwathmey if it was okay, so I was worried.

"They couldn't have been nicer. I think they were just glad to be outside, even though it was chilly enough that they needed their jackets. So it's not like there were flowers in bloom or trees budding or anything all that interesting to see out there. Fresh air, blue sky, and maybe thirty minutes when they didn't have to sit still and listen to me trying to coax them though their assignments.

"There were a couple of my classes that moved along the sidewalk and the paths in a kind of pod. I don't think they even noticed how closely they were walking with each other. Some boys jostled and bumped shoulders, and some girls linked arms —but the whole group of them maintained this physical proximity to each other that kind of weirdly thrilled me. Even the trouble-makers stuck close."

Ms. Hicks cleared her throat. "Cretia, I'm sure you know this, but I can't help saying that you can feel the planet tilt in Vermont at that time of year. At night it goes below freezing, then it warms up in daylight—which starts the maple sap running." As she spoke, Ms. Hicks berated herself for what she would ordinarily describe as inane chit-chat. She instructed herself to shut up.

But she didn't really want to. She wasn't going to just sit and listen to Cretia. Ms. Hicks knew her reputation was that she kept a tight lid on herself, with the only exposure of her personality occasionally appearing in a wryly phrased sentence of a document she'd composed. She didn't like attention, but she understood that she liked Cretia's slight grin and widened blue eyes focused on her.

"That's when the farmers start letting their cows out of the barn after they've been cooped up all winter. The cows gallop around and try to jump even though they aren't built for it. You can't help but laugh at them. But it's the horses that know how to celebrate a Vermont springtime. Sometimes you see them running just for the pure pleasure of letting their bodies do what they were meant to do."

"I've seen that," Cretia said. "I actually shouted, it was so beautiful." Ms. Hicks noted that the young woman was blushing, and then she realized it must have been because some heat and color had risen to her own face. *Now what have you done?* she asked herself grimly. Both women sat for some time without speaking. Mostly they didn't look directly at each other, but once or twice their eyes met.

"Shall I explain the severance pay?" Ms. Hicks's voice was low and soft. Some free-ranging sadness had come down on her. Living alone and not having a social life protected her from situations like this. It pained her to realize how she had kept yearning out of her life. And now she wanted to sit on a porch and shoot the breeze with Cretia until the sun went down. She felt lonely as a fence post.

"You don't have to," Cretia said. Her voice matched Ms. Hicks's in tone and volume, and her face was solemn. "It won't be much, I know that. I've only taught the one year." She bowed her head as if she'd confessed something shameful. "I probably shouldn't even have put you to the trouble of talking to me. To tell the truth, I don't mind being let go. I wasn't sure I could do it another year."

When Cretia raised her head, Ms. Hicks had to will herself not to look away from the young woman's face. "Franny Yates," she said, "came to my room after the last bell and asked if she could go home with me. All her teachers knew what the problem was—a stepfather who drank. But I knew she hadn't asked any of her other teachers before she came to me. She knew I was the only one who might take her in.

"Franny Yates was a junior and not a strong student, a kid who often went to sleep in class. But when I had them memorize poems I'd seen her take a wild pleasure when she recited John Masefield's "Sea Fever." This was a girl who'd never seen the ocean. She saw I was teary after she finished saying the poem, so after that she kind of locked into me, and I didn't mind. I thought I was helping her."

Cretia searched Ms. Hicks's face. Ms. Hicks let her look. Then Cretia grinned at her and went on. "Either way, yes or no, it was going to be the wrong thing. So I said no, and you know what that kid did? She recited the other poem she'd memorized, that Emily Dickinson one about hearing the fly buzz. Then she marched out of the room. That was it. Franny Yates taught me something I didn't want to know."

Ms. Hicks thought it ironic that she, who rarely left her office, was probably the one person in the whole state who could see why a great young teacher would be reluctant to return to her classroom. She was about to say that she understood, when she realized that Cretia was in this room just to make her decision real and final to herself. She could tell that Cretia had more to say, so she kept quiet.

"I'm a little ashamed that I've taken up your time. I'm moving back to Portland to live with my parents until I find a job.

I'll be fine. My parents are okay with what I'm doing and they're happy to help, but they don't get it. Same thing with my friends. *You loved teaching. You had a great year at your school. And now you don't want to teach anymore?* They act like I'm a failure or I'm still a kid.

"I haven't tried to explain it to them. I don't want to argue and don't want to have to defend myself. I came here because I wanted to tell somebody who'd know what I was talking about. So thank you for listening. You don't know me, but you've helped me anyway. I can stop worrying about what people think." Cretia paused. Then something made her face change—she looked stricken. "But I've used you!"

Ms. Hicks was glad Cretia said what she said, and it made her feel better about having been so affected by her. She considered saying, "Well, Cretia, I've used you, too," but she didn't want to have to explain that to the young woman. Or to herself. So what she did say was—and this was the most unprofessional sentence she'd ever allowed out of her mouth—"Cretia, your face is so red it could stop traffic."

Cretia's hands flew to her cheeks, and she squeezed her face as if she could make it stop blushing. The moment was a kindness to both women. There had been a second or two when Hazel had felt she couldn't keep herself from sobbing. But what came out of her mouth was enough like the sound of laughter that she was able to give in to it, and Cretia joined her. Both Ms. Hicks and Ms. Taft were still laughing when they stood up to shake hands and say a proper goodbye.

The Family Car

"It's almost a joke, John Robert. When you're growing up your parents' car is no more interesting to you than the refrigerator or the old sofa in the TV room. But then in high school the car suddenly becomes evidence of how out of it your family is and what a social outcast you are. When he was a junior your Uncle Walt actually got into a fight with a football player who said that our car smelled like baby puke. How the football player came up with such an insult is beyond imagining, and Tommy—your father—and I don't know why our brother had to take such offense that he very nearly got himself beaten witless by our school's starting running back.

"This was in the parking lot when kids were about to load up on the buses—your father and I were standing out there with everybody else. We saw Walt's nose start to bleed. We saw that the football player wasn't going stop—he was whacking Walt all over the head even though Walt had stopped fighting. So your father ran at the guy and blocked him so hard that his buddies had to catch him to keep him from falling onto the asphalt. One of those boys stepped up to Tommy, raised his fists, and started throwing punches, though not very serious or accurate punches—one of them landed on your father. Then the linebacker got onto his feet and started toward your father.

"That's when I dropped my backpack and ran right out there into the middle of the fray. That I was only fourteen years old, weighed under a hundred pounds, had never committed a violent act—and even the fact that I was a girl—none of that even entered my mind. I just ran out there and started flailing. All I can say is that when you're among idiots, you can become an idiot yourself. None of the boys I was trying to hit had any trouble dodging or blocking my fists, and so I yelled at them. I'd never really cursed anybody, so I couldn't find the right words.

"I screamed at them. I was crazy mad, and it didn't help any that the boys were just laughing at my efforts to hit them. All of a sudden I heard myself yelling, 'I'll tell you who smells like baby puke—it's you, Bobbie Puckett, and you, Jerry Dalton!!!' I pointed at them and screamed so loud it felt like my insides were going to spill out of my mouth. Then I heard this laugh from one of the jocks, and another couple of them laughed, too. I heard your father's laugh coming from behind me, and even Walt with his bloody nose was kind of snorting and trying to laugh. Half the school was out there laughing at me and all because of that old Chevy Delray in the picture. For all we knew maybe it did smell like baby puke."

LITTLE DOUBLE-BARREL

1990 — Burlington, Vermont

❦

HER GRANDMOTHER'S SHOTGUN CAME TO MS. HICKS BY WAY of her brothers, Tommy and Jack. They insisted she take it, she was pretty sure, because A) it was the one weapon of the family's collection they least wanted and B) they were amused by the idea of her having to own it. They both showed up at her house to deliver the shotgun in its tattered canvas sheath. "How do you know I won't sell it?" Hazel asked. They shook their heads and grinned. Tommy said, "We just know." Their smug faces made her seethe.

At this time they were all grown-up children, in their thirties. Their father had died some months ago. Now their mother was "downsizing," as she called it. She was ruthlessly purging the house of everything she didn't need. Hazel and her brothers were stunned by the energy and purpose their mother brought to the task. Hazel, the middle child, proposed that this purging was her mother's way of grieving. Her brothers shook their heads at her. "No," Jack said. Then Tommy said, "You're wrong."

Her brothers considered her a fruitcake. From early childhood they'd teased her beyond the limits of normal sibling conflict. They pushed her to the point of making her believe they'd always hated her. Hazel wasn't a wuss, but her brothers could usually make her cry. When they brought tears to her eyes, they'd stop their meanness for a little while. They had a list of the qualities of her personality that made her a fruitcake. Near the top was her contempt for what she called the "gun nuts."

Ms. Hicks thought she'd sell the shotgun just to show them. So when they brought it into the house she accepted it and served them coffee and chatted with them in her kitchen. When they left, she carried the weapon into her living room and took the thing out of its sheath. When she was a kid her father had taught her to shoot, but she hadn't liked it. This gun was lighter than her father's, but its shape and weight required her to use both hands, and the feel of it was a little disturbing. Standing with it felt awkward, so she sat down on her sofa with it resting on her knees.

Another of Hazel's fruitcake qualities, in her brothers' view, was her inclination to fall into reveries. Which is what she did sitting on her living room sofa with the shotgun in her lap. The first thought that came to her was that a gun is so specifically designed to kill or harm that human hands register its purpose the instant they take hold of it. Her second thought seeped into her brain like swamp water rising in a sinkhole. This was a killing instrument, all right, but her palms and fingers were savoring it.

Tommy and Jack had explained to her that their grandfather had purchased it for their grandmother, and so this was the lightest and least powerful of all shotguns. It had probably been advertised as "A Ladies' Hunting Gun," and their grandfather probably bought it from a catalogue. Tommy and Jack speculated that their grandfather had surprised their grandmother with it and that the old lady had turned her nose up at it. "It's in mint condition," Jack said, and Tommy said, "You know how Grandmama was."

In the minds of all three of them, their little grandmother was a woman of Biblical stature. She was sharp-tongued, outspoken, and powerfully opinionated. She had a collection of hatreds—communists, Black people, Martin Luther King, the entire Kennedy family, along with certain families and individuals of the local area. At one time Grandaddy Hicks had made enough money to enable his wife to live in a grand style, to have a chauffeur, jewelry, and clothes she ordered from Boston and New York. In and around Fork Mountain not many people had money, and those who did pretended they didn't. Ida Hicks was treated respectfully, even by people who despised her. Store clerks were so eager to please her that they seemed to lose their wits in her presence. Only when Hazel went to college did she begin to realize how the greater world might view her grandmother. When Hazel went to graduate school, she amused her teachers and friends by referring to the old lady as "my racist, flasher grandmother."

Evidently the shotgun in her lap was holding her in a state of meditating about her grandmother. Grandmama Hicks would love to see Hazel conjuring up such vivid remembrances of her. The old lady wore underclothing only when she went out in public, and even then a fancy slip was the only lingerie she could tolerate. Around the house or cutting roses out in her garden or walking around the property, Grandmama Hicks wore white cotton dresses worn so thin she might as well not have bothered with any clothing at all.

Tommy and Jack complained that Grandmama Hicks deliberately exposed her breasts and lady parts to them. Indeed anyone who visited or who worked in the house would likely have had to view the old lady *au naturel*. Every day in the spare bedroom upstairs she lifted weights and did calisthenics without clothing. She braced herself against a wall and stood on her head for at least a minute. She was vain about her physical abilities and enjoyed doing her exercises in front of her grandchildren.

The shotgun in her lap held Hazel in its spell long enough for her to review her grandmother's eccentricities in detail. When she had her grandchildren to herself, she quizzed them about their bowel movements. She examined their ears and reamed them out with a washcloth if they did not pass inspection. There was, Hazel had to admit, an element of entertainment for her and her brothers when they visited Grandmama Hicks. But they also walked over to her house because it made the old lady happy to see them.

If she were alone, Hazel made herself say aloud—or at least whisper—when her grandmother came to mind: *I loved you.* Even in death the old lady was ravenous for love. Hazel knew her brothers would cackle and hoot if she ever told them about her exchanges with dead Grandmama Hicks. *Yes, you loved me when you were a little girl and I bought you presents and gave you money for Christmas and your birthday. But now you're a grown-up. Do you still love me? Right this minute? Do you love me now?*

Hazel wished her brothers weren't such jerks so that she could ask them if they loved Grandmama Hicks. Giving her this shotgun they knew she didn't want was their idea of expressing familial affection. She looked down at the gun in her lap. There wasn't enough room on the sofa to set it beside her, so she placed it carefully on the stacks of magazines on her coffee table. She snorted at how out of place the weapon looked in her living room and addressed her grandmother: *You never even fired the damn thing. Why did you let them give it to me?*

℘

When Hazel first read the acronym OCD, she looked it up and lingered over the definition: *Obsessive Compulsive Disorder: Excessive thoughts (obsessions) that lead to repetitive behaviors (compulsions).* She realized the term applied to her, and she felt some disturbance from finding out that she had "a disorder." But she also felt comforted by knowing that there were enough other people like her that she wasn't the only OCD oddball on the planet. But here was the thing—she liked the OCD part of herself.

She was a step-counter, a clock-watcher, and a routine-repeater. She had a regular walk she took around town, a rectangle of three long blocks on the short side and six short blocks on the long side. The short-and-long of it amused her, and she'd counted the paces each side required of her. She also kept track of how many minutes and seconds it took her to walk each side of it. More than once she'd asked herself what difference these numbers made and who besides herself cared about them? *None and no one.* She rose from bed every day at 5:30, and she turned out her bedside light at 10:00. On Wednesdays she cleaned her house, top to bottom. For each day of the week she had an excellent dinner-for-one that was easy to fix and that she ate at 6. She washed her dishes and set them in the drainer in a certain order. She paid her bills on the day they arrived; she turned off the shower to soap herself up after she'd applied shampoo and conditioner; she tried to be one minute early for every appointment and obligation.

Over the years Hazel refined the way she did things, and she thought it was important to do them exactly that way. She visualized the assembly of her daily habits as a kind of outsider art installation. She'd indulged in and amused herself with the notion that anyone who could truly see it would consider her a genius. Now that she'd read the definition for OCD, she had to confront the idea that she was a fruitcake. *None of it makes any difference and no one cares.* And now there was this shotgun in her house.

❧

Because she couldn't make up her mind where to put it, Hazel carried the gun from one room to another. She got the hang of holding it balanced in one hand beside her thigh. She certainly wasn't about to take up hunting, but she thought it might be pleasant to walk through the woods with the weapon beside her like this. In the kitchen she set it on the table where she ate her meals. She noticed a box of shells on the counter by the door. Just like her brothers to sneak the ammunition into her house and not tell her.

She ate both her lunch and her dinner with the shotgun on the table beside her with its butt-end beside her plate. That night when she went upstairs to bed, carrying the shotgun with her, the thought came to her that, at least through her first day of owning it, the gun had become a companion. That idea would stupefy her brothers with happiness. She set the thing on her bed lengthwise as if it were taking its rest, then she felt compelled to go back downstairs to fetch up the box of ammunition.

When she came back upstairs and saw the weapon on the bed, she had a wild notion that it was a lover waiting for her. She decided that idea was sort of crazy, but it was also funny. She set the box of ammunition on her bedside table, sat down on the bed, picked up the gun to examine it, found the safety latch and the lever that locked the barrels in place. She pushed the lever, broke the gun open, raised it to look into its barrels. They were shiny and immaculate. Her bedside clock told her it was past her bedtime.

As if they were under someone else's control, her hands opened the box of ammunition, removed two rounds, rolled them in her palms, held them up for examination. The shells were thin cylinders, compact and cunningly made. Her fingers slipped one into each loading chamber, then she needed only a little strength to join the barrels with the trigger assembly and the wooden stock. When the two halves of the weapon clicked into place, a jolt of satisfaction snapped through her body and left her slightly dizzy.

Hazel was excited by the procedure she'd just completed and horrified by the pleasure she'd taken from it. Yesterday her only thought about guns was that she didn't want to be around them. Today she'd not only taken a gun into her house, she'd carried it around all day, and now she'd loaded it. Yesterday she was defenseless; right this minute she could shoot someone. She stood up, put the stock to her shoulder, and sighted down the barrels at the mirror across from her bed. She just touched the trigger.

☙

Instead of selling her grandmother's shotgun, she gave it a home in the corner of her bedroom closet. She'd removed the shells from the gun and put them back in the box. She stashed the box of ammunition in the back corner of a shelf, high enough that she could reach it but not without standing on tiptoe. When her brothers called her—as they did every couple of weeks—whichever one it was never failed to ask her about the shotgun. Hazel pretended she'd put it away and forgotten exactly where it was.

Days went by, then weeks, then a couple of months. She felt no need to take it out of the closet or even to check to see if it was still there. Already more than a hundred years old, it wouldn't break, decay, or collect dust. Its raggedy sheath was all it needed to stay clean and ready to use. When it came to mind, Hazel felt her mouth make its tight smile of acknowledgment that her life was different now. Yes, she was a single woman entering middle age, but she was also a person who could make a live person dead.

ᕗ

It's July and hot. When she returns from her walk, unlocks the back door, and steps into her cool house, she senses the thinnest current of an unfamiliar smell in the air. Hazel thinks maybe in a previous life she'd been a predator—she's caught the scent of an intruder and instead of being afraid, she's curious. Her pulse is up and so is her level of alertness. She closes the door behind her and makes no effort to be stealthy. She walks through her kitchen and through the dining room she rarely uses.

Ordinarily her living room is shadowy, but now the curtains have been opened, and a young man politely stands up in front of one of the wing chairs by the fireplace. "Hello," he says, in such a familiar tone he might be greeting a family member or a roommate. Hazel stares hard at him. He holds a book in his left hand, with his index finger marking his place in it. "You left your front door unlocked," the young man says. "I thought I should tell you that. So I came in and waited for you."

Hazel nods and makes a little gesture toward the chair behind him. He smiles and sits down, still keeping his place in the book. It's *The Second Sex* by Simone de Beauvoir, a book she read forty years ago, and she knows the exact place in her bookcase from which he must have taken it. His khaki pants and T-shirt suggest he's a student. He's clean-shaven; his hair has been recently cut. Nothing about him suggests criminal inclinations—which does nothing to make her less suspicious of him.

"I'm Gerald York," he says. "I know this is a little odd. But your door was not only unlocked, it wasn't even latched. I just touched it with my finger, and there it was, open as if you'd been expecting me and left it that way." Gerald York shrugs and flashes her a little what-could-I-do? grin. "I thought, well, I'll just step in and leave her a note, then I'll be on my way. But when I looked for a pen and paper, there was your bookcase and I'm a fool for books. I had to see what was on these shelves."

Gerald pauses, and Hazel lets the silence go on several moments. He murmurs, "I appreciate people who keep their books in alphabetical order." She stays quiet. Then she says, "Excuse me just a minute. I'll be right back." She doesn't exactly smile, but she puts on as polite a face as she's able to muster. Upstairs, she quietly takes out the shotgun from her bedroom closet, unsheathes it, then stands on tiptoe to fetch down the box of shells. She will not call the police. With the gun in her hands she'll be fine.

Hazel thinks Gerald York will probably leave while she's up here. She knows he hasn't told her the truth, but she also thinks he isn't here to harm her. She feels pretty certain he hasn't snooped around upstairs. If he wanted to steal something, the shotgun might be the most valuable thing she owns—at least from a thief's perspective. She breaks the gun open, takes two shells out of the box, inserts them into the loading chambers, and locks it back in place. Then she stands up straight, holds her breath, and listens.

Standing between the closet and her bed, she catches sight of herself in the mirror across the room. *Will I shoot him?* she asks the woman. The mirror woman tells her, *Yes, if you have to.* She has a moment of wishing she didn't own a gun. Over the years she has imagined and dreamed scenarios in which an intruder has entered her house. With her old dreams she always woke up just as the intruder was about to assault her. In her dreams since she's owned the gun, the intruder runs or else begs her not to shoot.

She checks the safety to be sure it's on. Then she goes downstairs, carrying the weapon in both hands. Gerald York is reading when she enters the room. *The Second Sex* falls from his lap, but he has the good sense not to say anything. She sits on the sofa opposite him, loosely holding the shotgun across her lap with both hands. They study each other. After a few moments he bends and picks up the book. Hazel sees that he's afraid and that he's trying to smile at her. "It's loaded, isn't it?" he asks.

Because his voice sounds only slightly fearful, Hazel respects him for keeping his wits about him. If she ever does shoot an intruder, it will be one of those blithering idiots who pee their pants and beg for their life. "Do you remember what page you were on?" she asks him. His face changes—he's surprised by her question, and she's glad of that because she is a little surprised herself. "I bought it and read it a long time ago," she says. "Not nearly as interesting as I thought it would be."

Gerald lets himself lean back in the wing chair. A notion of shooting him flashes through Hazel's mind. This would be a high achievement of irony to fire just when he's certain he's safe. She accuses herself of stupidity for conjuring up such a thought. "But you read it through to the end?" he asks. Hazel blinks at him and nods. Were they really going to talk about a book she'd meant to give to the library years ago? He leans slightly toward her. "I've read boring books," he tells her. "It's very restful. Like listening to New Age music. Or watching golf."

Sunlight beams through her open windows. Her neighbors are conversing nearby on the sidewalk. Hazel can't make out their words, but she can tell they're just passing the time. She's never had the patience for that kind of socializing. *If you're going to talk, then try to say something that matters.* That's her position. Even so, it pleases her to hear those familiar voices. Maybe that's what Gerald means by New Age music—something you can appreciate without having to pay any attention.

"Why did you come to my door?" She tries not to sound threatening, but the words themselves generate hostility. Once she's asked the question, she goads herself to be more assertive with this young man. Book-reader though he may be, he's also an intruder and a law-breaker. Evidently her hands are in favor of getting tough with Gerald York. They've taken hold of the shotgun so that if she does have a reason to raise the thing and point it at him, they'll be in the correct position to aim and fire.

"I do volunteer work for VPIRG," he tells her softly. "We're canvassing this neighborhood, asking questions to help us find out how people's everyday lives affect Lake Champlain." He looks directly at her as he speaks, but she is determined not to be taken in. She asks him how he can prove to her that he's telling the truth. Gerald smiles and points to a clipboard leaning against his chair leg. Which makes Hazel feel all the more foolish, because she hasn't noticed what has been in plain sight.

"All right," she says—and she can hear in her voice the agitation she feels. "But that doesn't explain why you walked in here. VPIRG can't have people working for it who just barge into somebody's house when they're not at home." She's aware of her hands tightening their hold on the shotgun. It occurs to her that if the shotgun had its way, she'd already be pointing it at him. She wills herself to relax. Gerald York probably means her no harm. He's just odd. Which explains why she wants to like him.

"VPIRG would send me packing if they knew I'd come in here. They'd be horrified." He shakes his head. "It's the first time I've ever done anything like this. But I've wanted to do it lots of times." He leans forward again, putting his elbows on his knees and staring intently at her. "I'm a sociology major," he says. "I thought sociology would be what I've always been interested in. How people live their lives. What their homes are like. What they do when they're alone." He pauses and shakes his head.

"Ms. Hicks," he says—and his using her name like this startles her. She hasn't said her name aloud. "Ms. Hicks," he says again as if he wants her to get used to his saying it. "When I was a little kid, preschool, maybe four or five years old, my mother used to take me with her visiting around the neighborhood. If she got to talking and didn't keep an eye on me, I'd wander into other rooms and have a look around. I'd even go upstairs sometimes. Then she'd notice and have to apologize and go find me.

"My mother was embarrassed, of course. She'd try to get me to tell her why I did it. I told her I liked kitchens and bathrooms. That was sort of the truth. In our family that became my famous answer to her question. Kitchens and bathrooms. But I didn't know. I was too little to know anything much, or to have the words for what I did know. Which was that it wasn't just rooms I liked. I liked being in them by myself. And without anybody knowing where I was. That's what I just adored. But I can't explain it."

Hazel knows what he's telling her without quite saying so. Gerald York is still the kitchens and bathrooms boy—which of course explains why he'd pushed her front door open and stepped inside. Her problem is that she understands all too well what moves grown-ups to replicate how they behaved as children. Hadn't she counted steps and kept every stuffed animal and doll and piece of furniture in her dollhouse exactly in the same place until she went away to college? *None of it makes any difference and no one cares.*

The only explanation is childish. It makes Hazel feel good to go to bed at the same time every night and it makes her feel bad not to do so. She can see Gerald studying her and probably figuring out that she understands him very well. But there is a difference between her secret acts and his. Her behavior doesn't affect anyone. The kind of fruitcake she is maybe irritates her brothers, but she does no harm. A thought startles her so that she speaks without thinking. "You're a transgressor!" Gerald flinches.

Gerald flinches, then he bows his head, and she immediately wishes she hadn't spoken so loudly and with such obvious glee in her voice. It's not polite or admirable of her to be pleased by the revelation that his behavior is wrongful and hers isn't. Even though they are similarly driven. She considers apologizing but stifles the inclination. She keeps quiet, and after some moments he raises his head and meets her eyes. Something is in his expression she hasn't noticed before. "Isn't that a loaded gun you're holding?"

Gerald's voice is soft, but his face tells her he's just landed a counterpunch. And she's felt it. "You've thought about shooting me, haven't you?" She'd known this was what he would say—she'd have said it, too, if she were in his shoes. "You could shoot me, isn't that right?" Hazel starts to shake her head, but she knows even that gesture won't be the truth. She takes a moment to try to calm herself and sort through her thoughts. "You don't know, do you?" he murmurs. "If you can shoot me." Hazel nods.

She's about to cry. Which she hasn't done for years. And there is no reason for it now. They're just talking. She wishes she could just make the shotgun disappear. She can tell him that thoughts shouldn't count against anyone, but she only half believes that. And he could see perfectly well that he's guessed the truth about her and that she's ashamed of herself. She's in such a state that she nearly blurts out that her grandmother was a transgressor and she'd loved the old lady anyway.

Gerald catches her eye and begins talking in a low voice.

She has to concentrate to catch up with what he's telling her. It's about a program he's heard on NPR. "So there's this therapist out in California who keeps knives in his desk drawer and invites his patients to hold them against his throat. These are people who are obsessed with the terrible thoughts they have. Like there was this man who couldn't stop himself from thinking *Murder my wife, murder my wife.* The therapist was treating him for it. When Gerald pauses to see if she's following him, she nods. "They had his wife on, and you might think she'd be upset to have her husband thinking about murdering her, but she wasn't. Evidently her husband had become dysfunctional because he loved his wife, but all he could think about was murdering her. She wanted him to get over it. So the therapist handed the guy the knife he'd had in his desk drawer and told him to check to see that it was really sharp and then put it right up against his throat."

"The therapist's throat?" Hazel asks. Gerald nods and then continues. "The guy doesn't want to, but the therapist persuades him by saying it will help him. He takes a couple of weeks to work himself up to it, but then he does it. Holds the knife to the skin right over the therapist's jugular, and it's okay. The guy feels like he's gotten somewhere. So the next step is he has to do the same thing with his wife. And it's the wife who tells this part of the story. They're in the kitchen, washing dishes."

Gerald pauses again. Hazel wants him to keep telling the story so she nods. Gerald clears his throat and goes on. "She's washing dishes, he's drying, so she hands him a knife. She knows about the therapy, she and her husband have been talking about it, so they both know the moment has arrived. She says, 'Go ahead.' He's scared, and she's scared, too. But he does it. Holds the blade against her throat. They stand there at the sink a long time. On the program they each tell what the experience felt like."

When Gerald stops this time, Hazel knows he's come to the end of what he has to tell her. "So he's cured?" she asks. "The husband doesn't think about murdering his wife anymore?" Gerald explains that it doesn't happen instantly or even overnight but that yes, the husband is over it, and he becomes functional again. Hazel says, "So it's kind of a fairy tale, isn't it?" Gerald smiles and says he guesses it is. "A fairy tale with a therapist in it." He nods. They sit quietly. Outside it's turning to twilight.

Hazel tries to hold onto the comfortable mood they've settled into, but more and more she feels it slipping away. Gerald won't speak first, he's taken his turn, and now it's up to her. "So you think—?" The face he turns to her is raw with fear. It pains her to see it, makes her feel a little sick. "I mean I guess we don't have to," she says. "I mean it's just a story you heard on the radio, right?" He doesn't move or speak, but his face doesn't change. He knows, and so does she. "Okay," she says. And stands up.

The thought comes to her that for both of them, this is their just punishment for living so long inside the cages of their lives. It's clumsy holding the shotgun with both hands as she steps toward him. She stops in front of him. Gerald tilts his head to the right. So she steps that way and asks, "Here?" He nods. She stands without moving. She's just breathing. Which is probably all he's doing, too. *We don't have to go any further than this* is her thought. But when he glances up at her, she sees terror in his face.

It requires tremendous effort on her part to lift the barrels of the shotgun so that they are pointed at his temple. *No further!* Her finger is on the first trigger. *Surely that's enough!* Gerald makes a noise, maybe a word. She thinks hard about it, processes what she heard. Two syllables. *Safety* is what he said. All right, she finds the little latch with her thumb and moves it forward. It's off. She knows she's crying when she tastes salt on her lips. She knows he's crying when she hears him sob.

Hazel wrenches her body sideways, screams, and flings the shotgun away from her as hard as she can. A millisecond later the thing hits the polished top of her dining room table and fires a blast that sounds like that whole half of the house has exploded.

Gerald helps her up from where she's fallen. In the stink and smoke they tiptoe past the weapon on the hallway floor into the dining room. Her grandmother's sideboard has had its doors blasted away and its collection of silver salt and pepper cellars mutilated.

When they investigate further, they find a hole in the back of it, and another in the wall beyond. They're half laughing and half crying the whole time. Hazel expects the police to arrive, but they don't. Nor do the neighbors knock on her door. *None and no one.* Cloth napkins are stacked on the corner of the sideboard. She takes one to wipe her face and hands another to Gerald. She blows her nose. "Forgive me for this," she tells him before she hugs him hard. Then she opens the door and lets him out.

Newspaper Clipping

Aunt Hazel set an old newspaper clipping down in front of me.
The black and white mug shot presented a baby-faced young man,
clean-shaven, with a recent haircut and a mouth that snarled at
the camera in a half-grin, half-sneer.

MAN ACCUSED OF MURDER, SEXUAL ASSAULT
IN TEEN'S DISAPPEARANCE

NASHUA — A Nashua man has been arrested
on suspicion of murder in connection with the
disappearance of a 19-year-old woman, and police are
actively looking for the woman's body.

Christopher Adam Wade, 26, is being held in the
Hillsborough County Jail in the disappearance of
Leanne Porter.

Porter was reported missing by her mother on June
5, according to the Nashua Police Department.

Wade is being "cooperative" in the ongoing
investigation and he's made a "statement," said Cheri
Hebert, a Nashua Police Department spokeswoman.

"He is helping with finding the body," Hebert said.

The court file on the case has been sealed.

Investigators were at Wade's home in Park Place
at the Clark Apartments complex Friday morning
looking for evidence. Several brown paper bags, taken
from Wade's second-floor apartment, were loaded into
a white, unmarked sports utility vehicle.

A man who lives directly next door said he didn't
know Wade and rarely saw him.

Wade's pickup truck has been impounded as
evidence in the case.
Porter lived in Northwood, and she was last
known to be visiting friends in Nashua, police said.
Wade was arrested late Thursday night and booked
early Friday morning into the Hillsborough County
Jail on suspicion of first-degree murder and sexual
assault.
He is being held without bond. His next court
appearance is scheduled Monday.

I was aware of Aunt Hazel watching me as I read through
the story. When I turned to her she met my eyes. I asked her if
she had had an encounter with this fellow. She nodded. "I was in
that truck," she said. "He had in mind to do to me what he did
to that girl. I might have been his practice run. I talked him out
of raping me, but then he said he was going to kill me. He was
this far away from doing it."

Aunt Hazel raised her hand to show me her thumb and fore-
finger a fraction of an inch apart. "He got right up to the edge of
doing it, but then he lost his nerve. Instead of killing me he threw
me out of his truck on an old logging road. That girl didn't get so
lucky." We sat quietly for a while. Then I asked her if she reported
it to the police, and she shook her head. "I should have," she said.
"It might have saved this girl's life." When I asked her if she felt
bad about that, she said, "Yes, but not as much as I should have.
I can't help being glad I've had my life. Seventy-some years of it.
I wish she'd had hers, too, but it's hard to make my mind take it
all in. The life I had. The one she didn't have."

We were quiet for a while. Then she said, "I've had a long
time to think about him, but I really haven't reached any conclusions. When he comes into my mind it's like he has some kind of
shield around him that blocks me from imagining what his life

was like. I don't believe he had any excuse for being the way he was. He wasn't all that big a man, but he was strong and mean. Maybe his mother abandoned the family, and his father beat him, but I doubt it. I think he was just a natural-born monster. Or maybe a self-made one. I've always thought I should hate him more than I'm able to. And if I can't hate him enough, then it feels like I should feel sorry for him. But I don't have it in me to do that.

"He was so despicable I can't even think of him as human. It was something that only looked like a human that shoved its body up right against mine in the cab of that truck with a knife set against my neck hard enough that I could feel exactly how sharp it was. Just a little twitch of that hand, and I'd have started bleeding like a pig with its throat cut. But then he let me live."

She moved her face a little closer to mine, almost as if she'd suddenly gotten angry with me. "Was he a human being when he pushed me out of his truck instead of killing me? What am I supposed to think about that, John Robert? Do you want to say that because he had mercy on me that made him human? But I'm the one who got punched and slapped by him, I'm the one he shoved up into that corner of his truck, I'm the one who smelled his stinking breath, and I say it was just that he lost his nerve. I swear I could feel it when he was about to kill me, and I could feel it when he lost the will to do it. Okay, I'll tell you what I think right this minute. When he pushed me out of his truck and drove away, he was already thinking, *Next time I'll do it right. Next time I'll fuck the bitch. Next time I'll kill her.*"

MS. HICKS RECAPITULATES

2012 — Burlington, Vermont

⁕

HAZEL EXPECTED HER LIFE AFTER SEVENTY TO BE WITHOUT upheaval. *I've been through some things* was what she'd whisper to herself when the spring days became so sweet she knew didn't deserve them. Or when the planet became overly generous and gave her sightings of cardinals, warblers, and the rose-breasted grosbeak. Or when her own cooking pleased her so much she had to dance in the kitchen just to express her gratitude.

But yes, she'd passed through heartbreak, bad health, self-loathing, despair that very nearly paralyzed her. The jobs she'd held had brought her little happiness. She'd suffered more insults than the average person. When she was nineteen, a man had put a knife to her throat, abducted her, told her he was going to kill her—then changed his mind, and shoved her out of his truck on a dirt road. She'd been through some things.

What Hazel did have from her troublesome life was inner resources. She had the patience to survive long sadness, the scar tissue to protect herself from hurtful people, and some skills to deal with her problematic self. She knew desire management was essential for maintaining daily equilibrium. She knew solitude to be a quiet companion always on call. In spite of having reasons not to be, she was mostly cheerful.

This particular year, however, her seventy-first, she was beset with nostalgia. Which wasn't like her. She believed in moving forward. Looking back was for people who had peaked in high school. The good old days was an alien concept. There was nothing she wanted to live through again. But now she had this yearning to visit with people from her past. What she wanted wasn't rational. She wanted it anyway.

Lucy Beth Groseclose from first grade. Gerald York, the young fellow she found sitting in her house one afternoon. Forrest Garrison, the man she'd lived with in New York for nearly a year. The homeless man she had called "her intruder" and sometimes "the rag pile." Felton Wadams, the boy who took her to the boxing matches when they were in high school. Pete Hoofnagle, her old boss the year she drove a school bus.

A component of Hazel Hicks's problematic self was that once certain notions had entered her thinking she couldn't let them go. The only way to deal with them was thinking them through to possible conclusions. So she invented scenarios for meetings with these old acquaintances. She started with Lucy Beth, who should have been easy, because all they had between them was a few months of sitting near each other in first grade. And a week or two of crazy joy playing together at recess.

Now Lucy Beth would be the same age as Hazel, but Groseclose most likely would not be her last name. A thought came to Hazel that made her snort: She could have coffee with almost any middle-class seventy-year-old white American woman and their conversation would approximate the one she'd have with a certified Lucy Beth. The real Lucy Beth might not even remember her. Or their playing together. Or their ecstatic recesses.

That they'd be strangers to each other now was a hurtful thought. *You remember how we played with each other at recess?* Hazel would ask. The woman would nod, and her eyes would tear up, so that for an instant Hazel would catch a glimpse of her childhood friend. *You remember how you wouldn't talk? How*

I asked you questions, but you wouldn't say anything? The woman would nod and look away. Hazel would whisper, *Did you know I loved you?* Lucy Beth wouldn't look at her.

Hazel felt like she'd been slapped hard. She hadn't quite realized her feelings could be hurt from something she just made up. First-grade Lucy Beth had been vivid in her mind for so many years that Hazel was helpless not to interrogate her feelings for the girl. So she sat at her kitchen table with her coffee and concentrated on how it would be to meet her old friend as a grown-up. Made it so real she could see it. And found out Lucy Beth had not cared for her at all.

Well, she could unlove Lucy Beth—not a difficult project. But it made her uneasy. Could the people she'd thought to be of crucial importance to her turn out to be completely different from the way she'd thought they were? That was very unsettling. She poured herself another cup of coffee and sat down again. Hazel realized she had no role model. She didn't know anybody who actually possessed what she wanted—an understanding of her life that would give her some equanimity.

Twelve-year-old Benny Sutphin had slashed her arm with his pocketknife when she was a school bus driver. Even now she could feel the burn of that. And Forrest Garrison had given her long afternoons of sexual pleasure that she would never forget. All these years she'd held them in her mind with a firm sense of who they were and what they meant to her. Now she seemed hell-bent on finding out what *she* meant to *them*. And in Lucy Beth's case, she imagined she'd gotten an answer. Nothing. Or nothing special.

But how could anybody live without kicking one's past awake and insisting that it talk, that it yield some useful insight? Because otherwise hadn't her life just dragged her through the years, tripping her up with humiliations, tossing her up in the air for brief pleasures, astonishing her, sorrowing her, angering, saddening, exhilarating her, with no pattern or point, neither reward nor punishment? Hazel was filled to bursting with all she'd lived through. Shouldn't it come to something?

At her kitchen table. Her coffee gone cold. A gray mid-March morning coming along, trying to brighten up the world outside her window. Hazel felt something coming to her, too. Her brain was carrying out its version of a spreadsheet, an inventory of her friends and acquaintances. Her brothers, her dead parents. She felt swimmy-headed—and even a little tired, as if she were catching the flu and needed to go back to bed to rest up for the illness that was about to take hold of her.

I can hardly stand anybody I know. She shivered with those words coming at her like a cold wind. The sentence would repeat until she could find a way to put a stop to it. This wasn't the first time such a thought had barged into her consciousness. But always before, her mind would take up the debate and persuade her that of course there were people she knew whom she admired and enjoyed. Pete Hoofnagle was one. Her brothers, Tommy and Jack. Her nephew, John Robert.

And of course there was her old theology professor, Dr. Norsworthy, a man of deep intelligence, strong conviction, and a shining code of ethics. But since Dr. Norsworthy was long dead, his place in Hazel's current thinking could only be that of an example of someone she had known and enjoyed and completely admired. But as to what he thought of her in the year she took classes with him? Didn't she have reason to think Dr. No appreciated the prickly questions she asked him in class?

Norsworthy once went off for ten minutes in response to her question about what Bonhoeffer meant by "cheap grace." That day she had thought he'd call her up to his desk for further remarks when class ended. He did not. Nor was he at ease on the two occasions she'd stopped by his office to chat. She really had to stop seeing him through the worshipping eyes with which she'd viewed him back then. In his eyes she'd been just another student. The final grades he gave her were a B and a B+.

Now that she'd lived as long as she had, Hazel realized that Dr. No had been a fine professor but probably not an extraordinary man. Nothing shocking about that—she could come to terms with it. Her coffee again going cold on her, Hazel received a bonus revelation from her kitchen table meditation. In her case, getting older evidently meant all her shining memories would be tarnished. She felt a sting of tears about to spring to her eyes over the loss of Lucy Beth and Dr. No.

It felt like she'd learned that two of the dearest people she knew had just died. Or to put it in the most brutal possible terms, she'd murdered two beloved figures she'd held in her mind for half a century. And all she was doing was just sitting here. Well, no—actually, what she was doing was examining her life, and wasn't that supposed to make her life worthwhile? It's true that she couldn't help herself and that there was nothing noble about her motives. Hazel snorted.

Maybe while she was on this track, she should examine the son of a bitch who had abducted her when she was a freshman at Crossley. Her memory of that guy was way beyond tarnishing. Except for the fact that he didn't kill her as he'd told her he intended to do. She didn't have a name for him. Which had never troubled her before. Nameless wannabe rapist-killer, why should he be graced with a name? Except that there was this: She sort of knew why he hadn't cut her throat.

She had told him she was having her period. So he shoved her up against the door of the passenger side of his stinking truck. He'd slapped and punched her a few times to make her stop fighting him. Even in her pain and fear, she couldn't let herself just give in to him. So he'd gotten this knife out of somewhere in the truck—a hunting knife she was pretty sure—and with his body jammed up against hers and his one hand pushing her face against the window glass, he'd set that blade up against the skin of her neck beneath her jaw.

She'd felt her heart beating right there against the sharp steel, a little throbbing sting. Whatever it was that had made her keep fighting suddenly let go, and her whole self went still. He felt it and knew he'd beaten her down. He pushed his face right up against hers so she had to smell his dreadful breath. He told her he was going to teach her something important, by which she knew he meant death. That was when she let her eyes meet his. She didn't know why. They stayed just like that a long time.

Then he made this sound that was like a woman shrieking. Instead of cutting her throat, he jerked the blade away from her, threw it behind him, somehow reached around to unlock and open the truck door behind her and just shoved her out of the truck like a sack of potatoes. She tumbled down head first, hit hard enough in the dirt and gravel to make lights start flashing in her brain like a pinball machine. He pulled the truck into the road, turned on his headlights, and gunned the engine.

Though she was aware of the truck spinning its wheels and fishtailing away, Hazel thought she was dead and what she was seeing was like the stream of final thoughts passing through the mind of someone who'd just been beheaded. All around her it was deep dark, but after a while she didn't feel the way she thought a dead person was supposed to feel. When she tried to move her hand, she found that the hand would indeed move, so she put it to her neck to feel where he'd gashed it.

It stung to touch the place, and she felt some wetness there that had to be blood. Now, sitting in her kitchen, she felt nauseated and needed to stand up. She stepped quickly to her bathroom and knelt over the toilet, just in time to throw up her coffee. For some moments she wondered if she was coming down with something. Lots of times she'd remembered pieces of that story, but she'd never tried to put it all together. She stood up, washed her hands, glanced up at the mirror, and shivered.

She blinked and spat in the sink. For a long time she'd hated that ignorant piece of shit so hard she'd have set him on fire if she had gasoline and a match. That feeling had never diminished in her for all these years. She thought maybe it was what kept her from being disabled by what he'd done. But there was another part of her, some soft and evasive little piece of herself—*whore Hazel!* —that wouldn't let her have hatred as the only thing she took away from that truck.

She put one hand on each side of the sink, leaned forward, and brought her face to within an inch of the mirror's glass. She'd never believed that old crock about the eyes being the window to the soul. But she did believe the human face can convey a lot of information about the person behind it. Information, however, was not what she and her abductor exchanged when their eyes locked into each other in that truck. "Say it!" she told herself aloud. *I wanted him to kill me.*

She'd never be able to say this aloud. It would never be a part of her consciousness she could accept. When he punched her and slapped her she'd had only contempt for him—and a desire to hurt him back. She knew she'd scratched him some, but she probably hadn't caused him much pain. Even so, even in her kitchen now, she was proud she'd fought him. But when he'd set the knife to her skin and their eyes had met, she'd just submitted. Which was why—she was pretty sure—he didn't kill her.

Most despicable was what she'd thought. Eye to eye with him she realized if he killed her, at least that would be something about him she could respect. Of course if she were dead, she wouldn't be carrying around the thought anymore. She gave herself an ugly grin in the mirror, shook her head, and returned to the kitchen table. It occurred to her that she wasn't the same person who'd sat in this chair a few minutes ago. Back in that truck again, she was shaky and sweating.

For more than fifty years she had had this monstrous chunk of experience all to herself. That span of hours in her nineteenth year had had more to do with who she was than anything else in her life. It explained a lot, she told herself. Not only did no other person know about it, Hazel herself had lived her life as if she didn't know about it. A late Saturday afternoon she'd walked downtown to Crossley Drugs—because she really was having her period and she needed supplies.

When she had stepped out onto the street—Main Street! —it was twilight, and her abductor was waiting for her as if she was his movie date for the evening. She'd never seen him before. "Hey!" he said, his voice weird but friendly. He'd taken her hand and almost immediately had it behind her and was forcing it up between her shoulder blades. Hazel yelped and shouted and frantically looked around for help. Main Street was empty as a tomb, and he was moving her to a truck idling at the curb.

It felt like he was going to break her arm off at the shoulder, and it took him only about twenty seconds to shove her through the truck's driver-side door and into the cab. He got in behind her, let go of her arm, and pushed her hard to the other side. He'd rigged that door so she couldn't open it, which she immediately tried to do. When she lunged toward him, he gave her a hard elbow to the ribs that knocked the breath out of her. Both he and his truck smelled like snuff.

He drove slowly out of town. Her window wouldn't open, and whenever she made the slightest move toward him he'd hit her with the back side of his fist. He made her nose bleed and her ear ring. From the outside they must have looked like a country couple driving back home from a trip to Hannaford's. At her kitchen table, she didn't want to remember any of this, but now she was seeing him all too clearly. She'd studied him so she could give the police an exact description.

Short and strong. Probably lifted weights. Wore sweats, the pants cut off just below the knee. High-top black sneakers, no socks. A baby face, clean-shaven, and a good haircut. A mouth that seemed stuck in a half-grin, half-sneer. He didn't look like a guy who'd drive a farm truck, and he didn't look like an abductor. Maybe a construction worker or a carpenter. He looked like a guy who'd have a girlfriend and a sex life. Fifty years he'd been lodged in Hazel's brain like a tumor.

The utter blackness in which he'd left her turned gray as her mind cleared. She could make out trees and shapes that stayed still so she figured they were nothing that would hurt her. When she moved to try to get up on her hands and knees, she figured out she was down in a shallow drainage ditch. Instead of standing, she crawled up through gravel and dirt until she was on the flattened out surface. She saw the gray path of the road going off in the direction she thought he'd driven the truck.

She wished she had a walking stick or something to steady herself with. She knew she couldn't crawl all the way back to Crossley. She stayed on her hands and knees awhile before she could persuade herself to attempt standing up. At her kitchen table, Hazel was suddenly awash in feeling sorry for that beaten-up girl alone on a dirt road in a night with no moon and no stars. She'd never before allowed herself to feel much of anything for the girl she'd been that night.

She felt herself rocking back and forth in her kitchen chair and heard herself moaning. Hazel wasn't someone who had any use for crying but in these minutes she finally gave in to it and let herself heave with sobbing. She'd never known the distance she walked or the time it took her. She remembered telling herself to stop walking—or limping and wobbling—and just to lie down beside the road and sleep. Something kept her going way beyond what she'd have guessed she could endure.

Hazel knew she was lucky she'd worn sneakers that evening and that she hadn't lost them in her fight with the abductor. She was lucky she didn't get lost in spite of never really paying attention to where she was going and moving her feet even after she stopped feeling them. Just as the sun was coming up, she saw she'd reached the edge of Crossley. Lights were switching on in the houses she was passing. Again she thought she might be dead and was having a dead person's dream.

The thought came to her again at her kitchen table. What she was reliving seemed possible only in a dream. She'd seen a paper boy on a bike up the street ahead of her, but he hadn't looked back. On Main Street the three traffic lights were blinking yellow, and there were no lights on in Parkway Diner. That's when she realized it was Sunday morning—nothing would be open until later in the day. But if anyone saw her now, they'd stop and ask her what had happened and could they help.

All the way to her dorm she remained invisible. Her keys were in her pocket, so she let herself in. No one sat at the desk. She walked up the stairwell to her third-floor room and unlocked her door. Her roommate had gone home for the weekend. Hazel took her clothes off, stuffed them into a plastic bag, put her robe on, walked down the hall to the bathroom, and took a long shower. Back in her room, she put on her pajamas, turned out the light, and crawled under her covers.

Finally now I can just be dead was what Hazel thought as she made her way toward the dreams that would come to her that night. The seventy-year-old woman sitting at her kitchen table savored the peace coming to the nineteen-year-old young woman in her bed. Such was the courtesy of doubt that had enabled both women to survive what their lives had decreed. Maybe none of it happened. Maybe the abductor and the truck were a bad dream dispatched from some toxic current far out in the galaxy.

But of course the young woman would wake sometime that afternoon. Her body couldn't have hurt any more if she'd been hit by a truck. Which wouldn't have been all that wrong. She'd look at her face in the mirror. She'd see the swollen places and the bruises. She'd see the scratches and cuts. She'd think there wasn't enough medicine in the world to make her feel better.

But then she'd realize she was hungry and walk to the canteen for something to eat.

When a girl gave her a second look on her way back to the dorm and asked her what had happened to her, Hazel found that she could open her mouth and speak. "You don't want to know." The seventy-year-old woman admired that answer. And something came to her then—she felt such tenderness for that young woman who gave that answer and who kept the nightmare to herself. The seventy-year-old wanted to give that young woman something so extraordinary she couldn't even imagine it.

It came to Hazel why she'd been saving Pete Hoofnagle for her final examination. Pete was the person who'd moved her beyond the abductor and his truck. Her boss the year she drove a school bus, Pete had escorted her into adulthood. He'd come to the hospital the day Benny Sutphin slashed her arm with a pocketknife. He'd let her keep the secret of what Benny had done. Against his better judgment, Pete respected her decision not to report Benny. That respect had steadied her all these years.

The abductor had disconnected her from the human race. And without even knowing what he was doing, Pete had fixed her. He must have thought of it as a small favor he could do for a young woman he liked. He'd given her that year of a bus full of middle-school children, chattering and fidgeting like baboons. Hazel drove those kids to school in the morning and drove them home in the afternoon. Some of them so mean they were probably behind bars now. Some so dear the world didn't deserve them.

With Forrest

When I sat down with Aunt Hazel at her kitchen table, she placed three photographs in front of me without saying anything about them. All three were of her with a striking-looking young man. In one they're standing in front of an apartment building, he has his arm around her, and my very young-looking aunt is doing her best to smile. In another they're sitting on a sofa, and again he has his arm around her, while she's staring at the camera with a look that I can only describe as suppressed hostility. The third is of their backs as they walk down a busy sidewalk; in this one, his arm is around her shoulder, and her arm is around his waist.

I arranged the pictures in a row in front of me on the table, but I didn't say anything because I wanted her to tell me about them without any coaxing from me. No one in our family had ever mentioned her having a boyfriend. My guess was that I was the only person she'd ever shown these photographs. The silence in that kitchen went on and on, but I was determined to wait her out. Finally, though, I couldn't resist turning my head toward her. She didn't meet my eyes. "These were taken while I lived in New York," she said. "While I was going to Columbia." I slid the first photo toward her with my finger just beneath the young man who has his arm around her.

There was something odd about his face, his features were mismatched or misaligned, but his smile could have won him a starring role in a movie. Aunt Hazel sighed but said nothing. I tapped my finger on the table beneath the fellow. She sighed again and said, "Forrest Garrison." After a pause, I tapped my finger again, just once and very lightly. "He and I lived in that apartment building behind us," she said. "We lived together for a little less than a year. It took me that long to understand that I couldn't love him."

This time the stillness of the kitchen became very loud, until finally she reached for the pictures in front of me, stacked them together and started to stand up. "But he loved you," I said as quietly as I could. She stood all the way up and held the photographs with both hands as if they might fly away from her. But she didn't step away from the table. Instead she stared out the window. After a while, she said, "Yes." And after another while, she said, "Yes, he did. And I should have loved him back. I don't know why I couldn't. He was perfect. John Robert, I confess that I sometimes take these pictures out and study them to see if they'll tell me why I couldn't love that man. And sometimes they tell me that I did love him but that I couldn't admit it to myself."

She continued staring out the window, and I had a moment of feeling what a powerful struggle she had carried out for her whole life. How to connect. How to survive if you can't connect. What I felt for her was not so much sympathy as it was admiration for the strength it required of her. Well, I knew everybody has some kind of struggle, but most people don't keep it to themselves the way my Aunt Hazel did. Most people find companionship even if it doesn't include love. Somebody to help or at least to witness what we go through. For most of us, it really takes at least two people to make our individual lives work at all.

A therapist most likely would have advised her to be practical, to stay with Forrest, to see how things went over the long haul, to give it a chance, blah blah blah. Since she was still there in the room with me, I knew she wanted the conversation to go on. So I told her I hadn't quite finished looking at the photographs and asked her if I could see them again. She looked down at me from where she stood and didn't hand them back right away. She appeared to be appraising me. I didn't blame her. Showing them to me in the first place must have seemed a dangerous step to take. She tightened her lips.

But then she set them on the table in front of me, arranging them one at a time in a row as I'd had them. Then she sat down beside me again. I moved the one I'd especially wanted to see between us—the one of them walking down the sidewalk with their backs to the photographer. I asked her who took the picture. "His mother," she told me. "She took all three of them. When his parents came to the city to spend a couple of days with us. And she mailed them to me. Not to Forrest." I asked her what she thought his mother had in mind. She didn't hesitate. "Marriage," she said. Then she smiled for the first time since I'd been there. "His mother didn't know me," she said.

I put my finger on the picture I'd wanted to ask her about. I told her that that was the one Forrest's mother must have thought made the case for marriage. I told her that the other two suggested that Forrest was interested but that she clearly was not. "I know," she said. "In this one my arm's around his waist, and so his mother must have decided we could live happily ever after. She should have looked more carefully. My hand is barely resting on his hip. I'm not snuggled up to him. There's a good two inches between us." I told her I thought it was more like half an inch. She snorted.

THE FORREST RECLAMATION PROJECT

2015 — Burlington, Vermont

❦

1. Because it ended as it did, with Hazel and Forrest agreeing that their emotional link had naturally evolved toward a severance—which is to say that in their final days together in the apartment each could hardly bear the presence of the other—and with neither of them feeling hostility or grievance toward the other, Hazel expected her feeling of loss to dissipate over time.

2. The concept of time, however, in Hazel's thinking about Forrest was probably deliberately vague, because A) he was the only person she'd ever enjoyed spending more than a few hours at a time with or had sex with more than once or thought she might love, depending of course on how one defined love, and B) Forrest had no competitors for an intimate place in her emotional metabolism, because she had come to understand herself to be unfit for romance or even chaste companionship, and she was not looking for anyone to replace Forrest in her life.

3. Which is to say that it was fine with Hazel for Forrest to have been her first lover—and she'd had only two in her whole life!

—though of course for Hazel the word *lover* was so problematic that sometimes for her own interior entertainment she changed it to *fucker*.

4. Which is to say that Hazel had accepted her lot as that of a loner.

5. So, months evaporated, then years disappeared, and then a decade or two dissolved into nothingness, with Forrest hanging no fire in her thoughts but with the coal of her remembrance of him dimming and brightening and never quite dying.

6. Sometimes it seemed to Hazel that her former selves, though each of them wore an earnest face, were so different and so distinct from her present self that they were strangers whose judgment was flawed and whose taste in fashion was downright silly but whom she recalled with some fondness and bemusement.

7. She never regretted Forrest.

8. Nor did she—in spite of the anguish it caused both of them—regret the end of her cohabitation with Forrest.

9. Spring of course—*stupid spring* she called it in her private lexicon—always brought certain vivid recollections hurtling into her thoughts like tiny meteors striking and very slightly harming the planet of herself as it orbited steadily toward extinction; e.g., her memory of the maddeningly patient attention Forrest gave to her nipples on summer evenings when their stuffy bedroom became too hot for bedclothes or covers, a ritual they performed in sweaty erotic glee, a state of arousal she achieved maybe three or four times in their months together, of desiring him only to continue the particular cadence of tongue diddling that her breasts craved at the same time other parts of her body became

so ravenous for his attention that she simply had to demand that he stop doing the one thing that she didn't want him to stop doing in order to do the other thing that she was dying for him to start doing, so that eventually she would have to take his head in both her hands and raise it from her chest so that his eyes met her eyes and she could whisper to him in a voice that was on the verge of screaming, "Don't you think we should move along now?"

10. Forrest as a graduate class she had taken in adult education was a tidy way she liked to think of him.

11. "So..." began a thought, her mind having happily felt a familiar shadow approaching—but because she was distracted or her powers of concentration could not gather sufficient focus, sometimes the particular person, the shadow owner himself, could not be adequately summoned, and the "so" would hover in Hazel's brain only so long before fizzling to darkness, which of course would require her to think about something else—the living brain being incapable of shutting off, regardless of the wishes of the brain's owner.

12. So, months slipped away, she lost track of the years, and suddenly the Age of Information surrounded Hazel, and with it came the happy thought that, if she were ever inclined to try to find out what had become of Forrest, she would not have to hire a private detective because her four-and-a-half-pound laptop computer and the Internet could very likely provide her with much of what she wanted to know about him—so then the questions became, *How inclined was she?* and *Exactly what did she want to know about him?*

13. If it was the tiniest ember of Forrest that had remained in her consciousness, then the possibility of finding him—and even

having contact with him—was like kindling, newspaper, and also the breath to blow on the spark that would produce as much fire as she wanted, which, truth be told, was only a little.

14. She was seventy-three years old.

15. In the online White Pages there were ten listings for Forrest Garrison in the US, while Google assaulted her with so many images of people of both sexes, all ages, and various ethnic backgrounds, and no physical resemblance whatsoever to Forrest but people who must have had some kind of connection with Forrest's name—there was even a Garrison Forest School—that at her desk Hazel found herself in a state of spiritual disarray, which caused her to put her laptop to sleep by closing it up, to sit with her head bowed, and to wallow in the shame and sorrow of being an old woman who'd been rendered helpless in her effort to use technology to locate, after half a century of having only silence and invisibility from him, the one and only fucker she'd ever truly known.

16. Though Hazel estimated she was likely to live another ten years, she doubted her wits would continue to serve her for more than about seven or eight years.

17. She was glad she would come to an end—enough was enough.

18. Yes, of course she had considered suicide, but in all her years she had yet to hear of an acceptable method.

19. In this desolate moment she was having with her laptop, Hazel amused herself with the idea that if she ever did figure out how to contact Forrest, maybe as her justification for tracking him down she could ask him to assist her in suicide—she would tell him that she could probably bear it if he would help her,

and she would explain to him that helping her would be an act of kindness not unlike that of putting down an old horse whose suffering would grow worse the longer it lived.

20. Well, she knew he would never say yes to that request, and anyway she wasn't really suffering, she wasn't that far along.

21. Of course certain pleasures were still available to her, two of which were essential, the glass of Kim Crawford Sauvignon Blanc she drank while she fixed her evening bite to eat and the salted caramel pretzel that was the glorious conclusion of her evening bite to eat.

22. Here was a line of thought that Hazel regularly inflicted upon herself in these days of contemplating making contact with Forrest: *He'll be an old man, just as I'm an old woman, and won't that plain fact just assassinate any possible pleasure I could take from seeing him or having a conversation with him?*

23. Willy-nilly a piece of information came to her, fell into her lap as it were—she was reading the *New York Times Book Review* in the Fletcher Free Library, as she did every Monday afternoon when everyone else had already read it, and on one of the back pages, in one of those little rectangular ads for books that were probably self-published, these words caught her attention: *Syntax as the Likely Solution—A Way of Life for the Intellectually Advantaged*, by Forrest Garrison.

24. The whole time she'd known him, he'd worked as an editor, and so of course she'd assumed that he could write capably, but she'd never imagined him as a writer.

25. Though she worried that it might reveal Forrest to be a crackpot or a lying schemer of some sort, she walked the two blocks

from the library down to Phoenix Books where she asked a clerk to order *Syntax as the Likely Solution* for her.

26. She herself was not a lying schemer, but she knew that a pretty good case could be made that she was a crackpot.

27. "Syntactical virtuosity is basically what distinguishes the human mind from that of an orangutan, an elephant, or a Beluga whale."

28. "Infinitely expandable, agile as the imagination of its user, lucid or opaque, generous or aloof, affectionate or cruel, syntax is the portal to the interior life of other syntax-users; however, writers who live deeply in the language eventually come to understand that consciousness itself sometimes seems to reside in diction and word order—which is to argue that syntax has its own life that is merely borrowed by its users."

29. What most surprised Hazel about *Syntax as the Likely Solution* was that the writing revealed nothing specific about the Forrest Garrison with whom she had lived during those long-ago months in New York, but reading it produced in her the kind of low-simmering excitement she had usually felt in Forrest's presence, as if the one person who could completely understand her mind and her body was this lively, witty, compassionate young man who completely adored her.

30. She felt foolishly certain that only the seasoned thought processes of Forrest Garrison could have produced this composition in the many years that had passed since he and she had stopped having anything to do with each other, which is to say that even if he couldn't have written it when she lived with him, an older, wiser, and more whimsical Forrest could certainly have written it.

31. Reading it, however, made her deeply uneasy—she was intimately with him; she was forever separated from him.

32. Halfway through, two ideas came to Hazel: 1) that sitting with it in her lap might be (and probably was) much more rewarding and pleasurable than it would be actually to spend time with the flesh-and-bones version of its author and 2) that there was some chance the person who wrote it was not the person she had lived with, some chance that Forrest Garrison was a pseudonym for someone whose real name was Jerome Harper or Jerry Watts or Ismat Dheer or even Priscilla Bahrman.

33. "To make syntax is to make sense of the universe and one's place in it, an ongoing human activity but also a basic human need as fundamental and inexplicable as prayer or song or sleep."

34. Every so many pages, Hazel would keep her finger in her place and turn the book over to read the About the Author paragraph: "After a long career in New York as a freelance editor, literary consultant, and ghost-writer, Forrest Garrison has recently retired to the Jersey Shore area where he plans to pursue photography, bird-watching, and his own writing."

35. The grimly smiling author had posed on a steep mountainside, looking up at the camera, with a winding trail behind him, a clever visual reference to the book's title, but the human image set off a disturbance in Hazel each time she looked at it. The man held his straw hat to his side, thereby revealing the oval dome of his shaven head. She could forgive him for losing his thick hair, but why was he presenting himself to the world as an outdoors person? The Forrest she'd known had been so incorrigibly urban that hiking up a mountain trail was the last thing he'd have done, and this face he pushed forward seemed to be deliberately hiding

the disproportionate and misaligned features that had made her catch her breath when she first saw him in the morning light of their apartment.

36. "Syntax is pliable—the order of the words can almost always be changed, the words themselves can be replaced, and the whole word apparatus (sentence, paragraph, stanza, chapter, etc.) can be deleted and a new effort can commence; therefore to compose a sentence is to summon hope, a readily available and notably more practical activity than attending a religious service, praying, or singing a hymn, but oddly similar in its mysterious promise—which is to say that syntax forgives, that syntax clearly demonstrates to every person who uses it that betterment is available, a fresh start is possible."

37. Hazel read the syntax-is-pliable passage several times before she closed the book without marking her stopping place. She carried *Syntax as the Likely Solution* into the spare bedroom where—though she'd kept the room neat and clean and washed the sheets and pillow cases every month or so—no one had slept during the thirty-some years she'd owned her house. She set the book on the bedside table, with its cover image of intertwining ribbons of language face up. She fussed with the placement of it on the table until she had it just right. Then she was free to leave the room. As she walked out something in her wanted to close the door behind her, but she'd always kept it open, so now she had to pause and think about it some moments. Finally she persuaded herself to leave it just open enough that a body could slip in or out of the room without touching the door or the doorjamb. Of course once she stood out in the hallway she had to decide where to go next—aside and apart from the question of what she would do when she got there. That decision she was confident she could make when she absolutely had to.

38. Her bedroom turned out to be her destination, and what she did for quite a few minutes was to stare at her impeccably flattened quilted bedspread, which informed her that even if she undressed and put on her bedclothes and got under the covers and pulled them over her head, she would not be able to descend into sleep, because sleep wouldn't accept her in her current state of mental chaos.

40. *I am going through something* was her first thought; her second was *Or else I am losing my mind.*

41. She made her way—*ambled* was the word that occurred to her—to the bathroom at the far end of the hallway, where she felt it necessary to pull the shade up and to open its one window.

42. It was a mid-morning of the second week in May, there'd been a series of thunderstorms through the night, and now the sky still roiled with moving gray clouds that occasionally opened to blue sky, then quickly closed again, all of the gloomy heavens infusing the trees and shrubs and lawns with a lemony light that through Hazel's eyes seemed to insist that she turn to face the mirror and take her clothes off.

43. She did.

44. Dropped them to the floor—an act she'd never before committed.

45. The glass version of herself took stock of the flesh version for a long while during which through the open window wafted in birdsong of such virtuosity she was certain she was imagining it or else this creature had recently flown up from hell to recite the tales it had gathered from the inhabitants of the fiery underworld: she stood still.

46. "This is what I've got," she told the old woman in the glass, hopping up and down and flapping her arms to emphasize the point—which sight made her laugh out loud.

47. If her heart stopped and she fell to the floor with her dropped dress, shoes, socks, and underwear—

48. "Ready for it," she said and showed her teeth to the glass woman.

49. Glass Woman showed her teeth right back at Hazel and told her what to do.

50. "Walk out of here and down the hallway.

51. "See that open door?

52. "Close it."

Chevy Delray

"This was 1955 and '56, John Robert, but when I think of it now it feels almost as far back as before the Civil War. On a Friday or Saturday after an early supper—while it was still daylight—our father would say it was time to go, and Tommy and Jack and I would run for the car, scuffling with each other to claim one of the seats by a door. I held my own with those boys, or I thought I did, because I got a door seat just as often as they did. But it could have been because our mother looked out for me. The scuffling had to stop when she got in the car, looked back at us, and decreed who got which seat.

"There was no arguing with her, even though we were all giddy, because our destination was the drive-in, which we loved better than anything else we did as a family. The movie we'd see would usually have John Wayne in it—he was our mother's favorite star—but sometimes we'd see a Jerry Lewis and Dean Martin movie or a Roy Rogers or Gene Autry western. On the way, our mother would turn on the car radio, so that we could hear 'My Heart Goes Where the Wild Goose Goes,' or 'Good Night, Irene,' or 'Dear Hearts and Gentle People.'

"There was Hester's Drive-In over toward Waterbury or the Sunset Drive-In halfway to Middlebury, and either way we went we'd drive two-lane highways over hills, past farmland, and roadside communities of maybe a dozen houses and a filling station that was also a small grocery store. When our mother would start singing along with the radio, our father would try to join in, and we kids would try singing, too, which was a little embarrassing—none of us could sing all that well—but in that car cruising through the twilight we were like a movie of ourselves, a movie about a lucky family in a prosperous country with a golden future just up ahead.

"I don't mean to sound bitter, John Robert. I had as sweet a childhood as anybody possibly could have. It was very white and middle class and small town. Naïve and simpleminded is probably the worst to be said about it. We had Korea and Selma and Vietnam and Iraq and Afghanistan ahead of us, and behind us we had slavery, lynchings, the Trail of Tears, child labor, and the Triangle Shirtwaist Factory Fire. In 1955 Emmett Till was murdered, and Rosa Parks was arrested. All of that and much much more, John Robert, but we Hickses just floated over that darkness like chimpanzees in a space capsule. I don't think we knew it then, but our carefree evenings at the drive-in were paid for by the hardship and constant humiliation of other Americans. My family's way of life was a delusion. The country that let us live as we did was a monster."

MS. HICKS IN HELL

1971 — New York City, Midtown

☙

GOD HELP ME, PEOPLE USED TO SAY. MAYBE THEY STILL SAY IT but I haven't heard it in years. And now I who have no business saying it find it hovering in my mind all day every day. Even as a girl I never thought of the deity as having a sex or being particularly human. I never doubted that something out there was responsible, but I was sure it wasn't anything you could ask for help. In my seventies now, I see god as a kind of science cartoon. A mass of pastel gases in different hues, a seething cauldron of divine belligerence and whimsy, with equal measures of pure meanness and blinding kindness. No gender, nothing like a human language, doesn't eat, doesn't sleep, pays more attention to beetles, koala bears, hummingbirds, and rocks than to the affairs of homo sapiens. Watches all of it like we watch TV. Turns it off and turns it on. Switches channels.

Moody, though—I could get behind a god who throws temper tantrums or falls into decades of a deep sadness that won't go away. I have stupid, stupid thoughts, a head full of them! I sometimes wonder if intelligence of any sort has ever paid a visit to my brain.

I who have always questioned the intellect of others now find myself doubting everything I think. Maybe the god I am so reluctant to ask for help configured us all to be idiots. Seven point eight billion stooges.

My nephew John Robert has probably prolonged my delusion, as well as keeping me alive, with his questions, his photographs, his contention that somehow my life has been exceptional. *About as exceptional as the house salad with ranch dressing*, I told him the other day and got a snort out of him.

I worry a little that I've encouraged John Robert to keep talking to me. When I've known perfectly well that the end of it will be not the pot of gold he's so determined to find but rather an empty old pickle jar.

Only a dozen or so people in my lifetime have found my conversation desirable. Of those I've been able to tolerate maybe five or six—and one of those was a dead man I chose to continue talking to for nearly a year after I read his obituary.

❧

When I was in my early twenties I lived with a man in New York. I left him not because there was anything wrong with him but because being with him magnified the awful things I saw in myself. He was probably the only person on the planet who could have put up with me year after year—and I think I knew that, but I also knew I couldn't stand who I was in my own eyes when I was around him.

After I moved out, I got pretty crazy and went into what I've thought of as my "Sound of Silence" phase. I listened to that song many times, but it was "The Boxer" that I fixated on. The verse of it about the whores on Seventh Avenue just kept ripping my heart out. For several months I was at its mercy. "There were times when I was so lonesome / I took some comfort there." I needed to feel the pain of it again and again.

I began to think about going down to that corner of Seventh and Broadway where I knew the prostitutes still snagged their customers. At first it was just one of my ridiculous ideas, especially because I was a woman. But given the breakup I'd just been through I definitely wasn't about to look to a man for help. And the worse I felt the more seriously I took the notion of seeing what a woman could do for me—a stranger and somebody who knew about hard times. I had a little money, I'd seen where they did their business, and it would easy enough to get there. What was to stop me?

I thought I might ask one of them—one whose looks I liked—just to go someplace and lie on a bed with me, maybe snuggle up and talk about our childhoods or what we liked to eat. I was pretty sure I didn't want to have sex with a woman, but I felt so alone it was like I had a terminal illness.

One Saturday afternoon I took the Seventh Avenue bus down to 42nd Street and the minute I stepped down onto the curb, I saw the prostitutes. Their outfits weren't subtle, and I didn't hesitate—I walked by the line of them and did it slowly. Even though I tried to catch the eyes of a couple of them—women about my age whose looks appealed to me—they paid no attention to me. So I wandered around midtown a little while and ended up going to the bar in the Paramount Hotel.

The sight of those prostitutes from close up—and there must have been fifteen or twenty of them, black, white, and brown—had riled me up in this peculiar way. My excitement was too general to be desire but it felt like desire's first cousin. I wondered if it would be so bad just to ask one of the prostitutes for sex and pay her for it and see what it was like. Even if the sex was horrible, I knew it would at least temporarily stop the lonesomeness that was making me crazy.

In the bar at the Paramount, I took a booth, nobody on either side of me, and when the barkeep walked over I ordered a whiskey sour. Good choice of a place to sit, bad choice of a drink. But that was okay, because it meant I'd drink it slowly. The place was dimly lit and quiet; there were only a few customers. I figured it was around three in the afternoon, a warm sunny day outside, as I remember it, though that bar was completely set off from the street—it was like its own little world. All it lacked was a jukebox that would play Simon & Garfunkel for me. If I'd been able to hear my songs, I knew I could unleash one hell of a good cry right there in that booth. But even without music, the place was just fine the way it was. It answered my need of the moment.

I became so absorbed in my thoughts that I paid almost no attention to what went on in the bar. The sadness I was going through had a way of narrowing the world around me and insisting that I pay attention to it and it alone. People came, people went, while I stared at my hands, reviewing the faces and the outfits of the women on Seventh and Broadway. I kept remembering how purposeful they'd been in ignoring the signals I'd tried give them. *No come-on for you, my dear,* was what their manner had conveyed.

I was savoring my misery, which I was sure was the worst I'd ever experienced. I wasn't hurting quite bad enough to try to get in touch with the man I'd been living with, but that thought did cross my mind. I knew he'd come if I called, but I definitely didn't want to pick up our old life again. I didn't feel like apologizing for leaving him, and I didn't want to see disappointment in his face—ever again.

"May I join you?" said a man standing beside the booth. He seemed to appear from nowhere, and he startled me, even though he'd kept his voice soft and stood a polite distance away. I looked up at him, the words *No, thank you*, making their way down from my brain and up out of my chest. *He's old*, was what my eyes told me, and I suspect that fact alone stopped me from saying anything at all to him, at least for a moment. Instead, I let my eyes pass down over his clothes and back up to his face in what he must have considered a brazen way.

He wore a gray suit, a navy blue tie, a white shirt, and shiny black wingtips. He was clean-shaven and his silvery hair had been recently cut. So this was a businessman who had an understated polish in his face and the way he dressed. Not quite handsome, probably in his early sixties, he looked like a man who was accustomed to being treated with respect.

My trance of misery and mild general arousal still had its hold on me, and I knew it would be ever so easy to send this man on his way. *Thank you, sir, but right now I need to tend to my loneliness.* I was on the verge of saying something like that when I suddenly saw myself through his eyes.

I'd been silly enough to wear a dress that was more maroon that it was red but that was sleeveless, that fit me nicely at the neck and shoulders, and that modestly presented the little bit of bosom I had to offer. I'd picked my outfit with the aim of making an impression on the Seventh Avenue ladies, but clearly it had not impressed a single one of them enough to meet my eyes as I'd walked past them.

The man I'd lived with once observed that I had a Sunday school sexiness about me, a remark that pleased me. It was the closest anyone ever came to saying that I was sexy or pretty or good-looking or cute or any of those terms. *Beautiful* and *terrific* had always been out of the question, but I'd often wished for a word or words that went further than the *nice-looking* my parents awarded me all through my teenage years and that a boy named Felton Wadhams was rumored to have said of me in high school.

At an early age I'd reconciled myself to the fact that my physical appearance did little to recommend me. So I wasn't surprised that the prostitutes had paid me no mind. But evidently the way I'd tricked myself out for them worked for at least one person in the city, and here he was politely asking for permission *to join* me. I almost snickered at the term, which I was sure he hadn't intended in a lascivious way.

It was a what-the-hell moment, of which I'd had probably fewer than half a dozen in my life, and most of those I've refused. Something kept me from speaking, but the private joke I'd made of his word-choice helped me put a tight grin on my face, and I lifted my hand in a little welcoming gesture toward the seat opposite me.

The man maneuvered into the booth—with some grace—folded his hands in his lap, and straightened himself a bit, all the while not looking at me. After a moment of settling himself, he raised his eyes to mine, so that I had an instant of thinking he'd noticed how carefully I'd scrutinized him.

"Joe Arnold," he said. He had the good judgment not to extend his hand toward me. And not to smile.

"I'm Hazel," I told him. My smile was long gone by now. In fact I felt a jolt of wishing I hadn't let him join me. I wanted my loneliness back—I knew it would give me no trouble. I leaned back and gave him the least friendly face I could come up with.

Joe Arnold nodded, as if to acknowledge my bad attitude toward him. Then he looked over at the bar and around the room. I thought maybe he was checking to be sure that I was the best company he could find at the moment.

When the barkeep appeared, Joe Arnold asked for a Coca-Cola for himself and a fresh drink for me. I told the barkeep that the whiskey sour wasn't working for me, and I asked him to recommend something. When he said he made a really good Rusty Nail, I told him that sounded like just the drink I needed.

After the barkeep was out of hearing distance, Joe Arnold told me he knew better than to start drinking this early in the afternoon. I told him that I wasn't much of a drinker at any time of the day.

Then we sat and regarded each other while we waited for our drinks to arrive. I thought that when we did speak we might both say in unison, "So what are you doing here?"

That wasn't how it went. The barkeep set down our drinks and went away. We let our glasses sit untouched. And I liked it that Joe Arnold didn't seem to know what to do or say in the silence. I was fine with neither of us saying anything. Maybe this would be all there was to it, an afternoon of sitting in this booth, occasionally taking sips from our glasses, and saying nothing. Just sitting in proximity with each other.

"You first," he said.

"What?" I said.

Then he nodded. He knew I knew what he meant.

I did know. I also knew that no matter what I told him, he probably wouldn't challenge it. He just wanted me to tell him something. Or make some noise. I could have hummed "She'll be Coming 'Round the Mountain," and he'd have been grateful. So I thought I would see how much of the truth I could pry out of myself. I felt reckless. What did I have to lose?

"I'm originally from Vermont. I'm doing graduate work at Columbia. I've just moved out of an apartment I've been sharing with a man for the past year. And now I'm really hurting." I paused between sentences and said each of the sentences slowly while looking directly at Joe Arnold. "I can't seem to adjust to living by myself," I told him. I was certain I'd said more than I should have, but I didn't care. I'd liked hearing my voice deliver those solid facts to another person. I was proud of myself for having stuck to the truth.

Joe Arnold had stared at me while I spoke and seemed to absorb each statement as I made it, but now that I was finished, he looked away. I thought maybe he was blushing and I wondered if I'd embarrassed him.

"I'm sorry for what you've been going through," he said.

Whether or not he meant it, I appreciated the sympathy. I nodded.

Then he couldn't seem to bring himself to speak. I was determined not to say another word until he took his turn, but he seemed paralyzed. I noticed that now he was indeed blushing. For a minute or so I thought he might simply stand up, apologize, and walk away.

Finally he shook his head and raised his eyes to meet mine.

His face was slightly contorted. "I want to leave my wife," he said. The words erupted out of his mouth in way that made them sound like *I think I'm going to throw up.*

I wasn't horrified. I tried to be sympathetic since I knew what it felt like to leave somebody. I made myself say, "I'm sorry." He probably heard the truth I wasn't saying: *I wish I could feel your pain, but I can't.*

"I can't imagine you'd want to hear the details," he said.

I nodded. He was right—I didn't.

"I haven't ever said it aloud," he murmured. "Maybe that's all I needed to do. Get it out there where somebody could hear it."

I blinked at him. Our conversation seemed to be moving us farther and farther away from each other.

"If you want to, you can leave," he said, his voice very soft. "I'll pay for our drinks."

I didn't know what I wanted to do. And didn't know what to say. So I stared at him with what had to be a very foolish face.

"I probably would, if I were you," he murmured. "Leave," he said. His expression was a weird combination of shame and relief. Truth be told, I preferred this look on his face to the tight-and-in-control version of himself that he'd presented when he asked to join me.

So I smiled at him. Or rather I realized that I was smiling at him—I hadn't exactly decided to do that.

He seemed to relax then. "Look," he said, leaning forward, clasping his hands together on the tabletop between us. "I asked to sit with you because I thought maybe I could persuade you to let me get us a room. I thought we could go upstairs and spend some time together. I guess I hoped for sex. Sure, I should just say so. Because you'd know even if I didn't say it. I'm sorry if you're insulted. It's taken me a little while to understand that you weren't sitting here by yourself because you wanted company."

I heard what he said and understood him perfectly well. And having recently cruised the line of Seventh Avenue whores hoping for a come-on, I could hardly be insulted. But I couldn't put everything together in any way that helped me know what to say or do. I didn't want to go upstairs with him—maybe just because I couldn't imagine how it would go once we closed the door and stood in the room with a bed directly in front of us. I didn't want to take my clothes off, and I definitely didn't want to see Joe Arnold naked. But I also didn't feel like standing up and leaving the bar. And I didn't want to go on sitting in that booth by myself.

I wished I could just beam myself out of there, but then I realized I couldn't think of a destination.

I closed my eyes and thought maybe this was the lowest moment of my life.

I kept my eyes closed until I was sure I wouldn't cry if I opened them. The thought occurred to me that maybe Joe Arnold would take the opportunity to leave some money on the table, slip out of the booth, and head for the door. But when I opened them, he was still there.

And he was putting money on the table in front of him.

So he's about to leave was my thought. I felt myself blushing. Out of some weird sense of decorum I didn't look at the money.

I watched his face while he put his wallet away. He looked relaxed now, a little pleased with himself. I didn't blame him. He'd hoped I'd be somebody other than who I was. I had often hoped the same thing.

"Yours," he said, tapping the table.

Lined up like Monopoly money were four one-hundred dollar bills.

He saw my shocked expression. It made him smile. "Yours," he said again.

I couldn't keep my eyes from glancing out through the lobby toward the elevator—the Paramount was a one-elevator hotel.

He chuckled. "No," he said. "It's not for that. It's just that I could have gone the rest of my days without ever saying aloud that I want to leave my wife. If you hadn't been here. If you hadn't let me sit with you. If you hadn't said what you said, I'd have never gotten those words out."

I know I looked down at his money again, and my expression must have been really comical, because he laughed out loud.

"Look," he said, "I just realized this. I may never leave my wife—I almost feel like now that I've said those words, I don't need to leave her. But whether I do or not, you've saved me thousands of dollars I won't have to pay my therapist if I keep on going to see her. Which I'm pretty sure I won't."

I stared at him. I wanted to feel like he felt. Free of something. Out from under this loneliness that was like a bully waiting for me every morning when I woke up!

"Yours," he said.

It was the third time he'd said that word, and what struck me then was that maybe he didn't know it, but this man was trying to buy his way out of hell. I wasn't offended. In fact I was sort of thrilled. It came to me then that maybe I could make the deal work for both of us. I sat up straight.

"I'll take it," I said. I picked the bills up one at a time, all the while looking him straight in the eyes. I took my time because I was excited by what I was about to tell him.

"But I want to go upstairs," I said.

His face changed. He actually looked a little afraid.

"With you," I said.

He flinched.

"You and I, Joe Arnold," I told him. "We're going up there."

⁊

I was a lot worse off than I realized that day in the Paramount Hotel fifty years ago. And Joe Arnold was just as bad off as I was. He had no idea what a deep pit he'd been living in for years. Maybe that ignorance is a mercy of some kind or else a survival component that comes with the human apparatus. Like those soldiers who get shot up so bad they can't live more than a few minutes thinking *Hey, this isn't so bad, I'm going to be fine.*

I've come to believe that relentless pain can sometimes be a help to you. It humbles you, it realigns you with your brother and sister human beings, and it prepares you to be healed if you can find your way to something or somebody that can fix what's wrong with you. Maybe non-stop hurting even guides you to that right something or somebody. I've come to think of loneliness as a kind of corrective angel. My deity of the pastel gases and the seething cauldron might dispatch such an angel to nudge a human creature who needed to be turned in one direction or another.

❧

Joe Arnold and I got our clothes off pretty quickly in that room. I'd had no faith we could get that far without one or the other of us saying *I can't do this* and walking out. But we didn't turn on any lights as we walked through the door, so what we had was just the late afternoon sun beaming through the window shade. Probably if I'd had a look at Joe in better light, I'd have been put off by what age had done to his body. I don't think he'd have been put off by the truth of my body, but he also would have seen very little to convince him he should have come to that room with me.

A meticulously made-up big bed is a beautiful sight, a beacon of comfort, a reminder that respite is possible. We sat side by side on it and took our shoes off. From there the bed gave us permission, so that getting naked was easy. Joe and I had no problem making our way into that bed. From opposite sides we hopped under the covers like sixteen-year-olds. Clean, ironed sheets whisper sweet messages to almost anybody's skin.

All right. About the sex—clumsy and funny for a while, then turning sad when it looked like we weren't going to be able to make it happen. I think we both had thought failure was inevitable, and I don't know about Joe, but I would have been in seriously awful shape if I'd had to walk out of that room without even being able to have intercourse.

Joe propped himself over me while we both struggled to get him inside me. Finally, when I knew he was about to give up, I told him to let me get on top and try something else. I asked him to turn with me, and I said please. Desperation can improve your manners. Something had transpired in those minutes of his trying so hard and wanting it so much and failing. Just plain old flat-out failing. So I knew it was up to me, and at that point when we had every reason to be angry at ourselves and each other I think we both saw that kindness was really our only option.

I nudged him over, and I rolled with him so that for a second or two we were the beast with two backs. On top of him I snuggled in, I tried to get my belly and chest as close to his as I could, and I had my head on his shoulder so that my mouth was right up to his ear. This was a way of lying together that I'd never experienced with the man I'd lived with, though I'd always meant to ask him if we could try it.

I talked dirty to Joe. Or rather I whispered dirty to him. And my level of talking dirty was probably about that of a seventh-grader. I told him I was really, really wet. Which wasn't true. I told him I wanted his cock. Which was true. I told him my nipples liked the hair on his chest. And I moved my skin on his skin while I said these words—and some others—again and again in his ear. I licked his ear, too, and I'm pretty sure that's what woke his cock up. I sensed it down there, and God help me I felt like I was his voodoo princess. "I'm your whore, Joe," I said. "I want your cock, and I am most definitely your whore."

Okay, I don't think either one of us thought we'd make it as far as a climax. For damaged people like we were it would probably have been okay if all we could manage was intercourse without orgasm. Not ideal but better than nothing.

Maybe you think it is crazy and inappropriate for a woman in her seventies to talk this way. But I have something else to say, and it's maybe the most useful observation I have to offer. Suffering can teach you how to say and do what's necessary, and even then maybe all you'll get out of it is more suffering. But doing and saying what's necessary can sometimes—maybe just occasionally—take you to the other side of your anguish.

So Joe and I miraculously accomplished the act of penetration. When I felt him holding his breath, I realized that was what I was doing, too. We were right at that point of understanding we might not have more than a minute or two of being properly and happily joined. The moment felt really precarious.

"I'm your whore, Joe," I whispered. I swear to the god of divine belligerence and whimsy that my sex registered his sex gaining what I'll call conviction. So our bodies were doing their best to take us where we needed to go. "What are you?" Joe asked in a kind of rasp-whisper that startled me with his mouth so close to my ear. I told him what I was. And when he asked again, I told him louder.

It came on us fast—like maybe seven minutes. I could feel Joe moving way too quickly for me, and just about the time I was about to tell him to stop or at least slow down, he bucked and grunted and trembled, so that my body spoke back to his body with a couple of contractions that brought a little shout up out of my chest. It barely qualified as an orgasm, but I never had one that made me any happier.

I stayed on top of Joe until I could feel him wishing I'd get off. So I did. And we lay on our backs for a while. Then he turned on his side toward me and said, "You know what?"

I turned on my side toward him, put my hand on his chest, and said, "What?"

I watched him getting his words straight in his mind. Then he said them slowly. "I didn't even know I was dead. And now look what you did to me."

I didn't really want to, but I knew I had to cry, and so I just let myself go. And Joe Arnold, bless his heart, just scooted up close and hugged me and let me keep crying as long as I wanted to.

❡

Okay, half a century later, I'm the same fool I always was. Except that I don't live in hell anymore. What I did with Joe Arnold in the Paramount Hotel was nothing I ever wanted to do again. I might have thought of doing it if I'd ever gotten that deep down into sadness again. But I didn't. I got back on track and I've more or less stayed there. I don't think I lowered my self-esteem because of what happened in that room, but I did find it much easier to see qualities in other people that made me respect them. I guess that's what Joe Arnold taught me. If I had to say what I've learned from what I hope has been a thoughtful life, it might be just that. Finding ways to respect other people makes me happier with myself. I'm a natural born fault-finder, so respect isn't easy for me. But I've got this voice I sometimes hear when I need it, and I listen hard. *What are you, Hazel?* I'll hear. And I know the answer. *I'm your whore, Joe. I'm your little whore.*

Decorous Old Gent

My first thought was that she left this photo on the kitchen table by accident. It was summer, and she'd just called to me from upstairs to let myself in. I stepped through the screen door, walked into the kitchen, where the water for our tea was simmering on the stove. And there was a photograph I hadn't seen before—and one that must have been taken recently. In it an elderly fellow with a moustache and dressed in a jacket and tie smiled at me somewhat mischievously. My second thought was that this was how she'd intended us to meet. She gave me plenty of time to study the picture. I was pretty sure I'd seen him around town.

"Kent Peltier," she said when she came in the kitchen and sat down with me. "He was the director of special collections up at the library until he retired last year. He says he hardly realized there was a world out here until he stopped going to his office. He volunteers at the Fletcher Free Library now—that's how I met him. He helped me find the DVD of a movie I wanted to watch, *The Quiet Man*, and then he checked it out for me at the front desk." Okay, so I knew she wouldn't have told me about Kent Peltier if he hadn't made a positive impression on her.

I couldn't remember the last time my Aunt Hazel had mentioned anybody who lived in town. As far as a network of people who were close to her, I was it—and I was the only relative she could tolerate for more than about five minutes. "He talks too much," she said, putting on a face to show me that she was judging him critically. But I'd learned to read her expressions well enough to see a little smile hovering behind her severity. "His problem is that he knows too much, and he doesn't have anybody to talk to. He reads the *New York Times* cover to cover every day and three or four journals as soon as they come out."

I said that Mr. Peltier's conversation must be really interesting. "Well, yes it is," she said, "but then it's also boring, and sometimes it's both interesting and boring. When he gets going, I want him to shut up, then when he's quiet, I start wondering what's wrong." This was a moment I won't forget from my long relationship with my aunt—she was flustered by her own words, and I thought she might be blushing. I was quiet for a bit, and then I said that maybe she could coach him in how to talk to her in just the right amount. "Maybe so," she said and looked toward the window. I asked her when I would get to meet Mr. Peltier. She turned to me, as if I'd said something inappropriate. "It's too soon for that," she said sharply. But then she murmured, "I'll let you know when it's time."

SWALLOWS

1952 — Burlington, Vermont, Rock Point

❧

HIRED SPECIFICALLY TO TEACH "PAPER, CLAY, WOOD, AND Cloth," a class in basic craft skills, to eight- and nine-year-olds, I was sixteen when I worked as a counselor/teacher at the Rock Point summer camp. Even though I didn't like having to ask my campers to call me Miss Wilson, it was the best job I've ever had.

My mother had put me up for it without consulting me first, probably because she knew I would ask her not to. She did so because she knew I had a passion for making things—crafts—but also because when she was my age she had taught a similar class at Rock Point.

Her secret agenda, however, was that my anti-social inclinations had begun to concern her, and she thought the job would require me to engage with other people. Had she explained her reasoning to me, I would have said something along the lines of "Mother, are you sure children that age qualify as people?"

Of course her answer would have been, "Claire, when you were that age, were you a person?" From when I was about seven, my mother and I had been locked into what we jokingly called "our affectionate struggle."

Being obnoxious was not my only defense against her, but it was a pretty good one. My mother was smart, articulate, and patient, and her love for me was a potent weapon; however, she

189

had an emotional allergy to me when my mood turned spikey.

I was only briefly obnoxious about the job—and I couldn't help being pleased when the summer camp staff invited me to join them—because I already knew Rock Point to be an uncommonly good place. Good in the sense that it was situated on about a mile or so of the Lake Champlain shore, that it had many woodland paths, and that it seemed to me to be infused with that loosey-goosey Episcopalian free-style take-me-as-I-am spirituality.

Also throughout my childhood the place had never failed to improve my mood when my mother took me to Rock Point, which was whenever she felt restless and in need of what she called "a change of scenery." For my whole life my mother has flirted with becoming a priest—though I doubt there's any cause and effect between my birth and her religious yearning.

When I signed the contract for the two-month position, I suddenly understood that it was a bigger deal than I'd thought it would be. I'd never been employed before, never even imagined being paid for my ability and my time, and certainly never signed a document that listed duties I had to carry out whether I felt like doing so or not.

If I felt a little trapped, I also felt peculiarly grown-up. My parents seemed to notice a change in me and to treat me as if I'd suddenly become a more responsible person, and I was mildly thrilled that they were giving me more respect.

My classroom was barn-like, large enough for two or three times as many children as I'd be teaching, with a high ceiling and one wall with a table-like shelf and a row of permanently sealed windows along its length. Always cool in the mornings, that workspace became warm enough on sunny days to make the campers and me sweaty by mid-afternoon.

The room had a baked cedary smell that suggested it was where work of some kind—maybe carpentry or furniture-making?—had been accomplished in the past. It held six rectangular tables that I arranged in a square with a dozen chairs around it, though I rarely had more than ten children in my classes.

Bobby Wilson, Hershel LeTourneau, Hazel Hicks, Rachel Telford, Pete Copenhaver, Penny Hale, Elly Clay, and Katie Randall were my morning class, and those children have remained vivid in my thoughts for all this time. When their parents brought them into that huge room to meet me, they seemed so small and shy and dear that I was instantly smitten with them.

Each child came to me, with the parents herding him or her in my direction, and I shook their hands formally, as our camp director had suggested I should. I was pretty sure that most of them had never suffered through the ritual of shaking an adult's hand.

During that first meeting with my campers, I was jolted by the realization that I suddenly considered myself to be an adult. To be specific, it was Pete Copenhaver's small, sweaty hand in mine (after his father whispered to him that he should extend his hand toward me) and his reluctance to look me straight in the face that made me imagine myself through his eyes.

I wasn't so happy with that news. For a little while that morning I would have been okay with changing places with any one of my campers.

The one to whom I'd have chosen to hand over my responsibility was Hazel Hicks, whose somber face and bold eyes meeting mine—dark brown eyes that continued to scrutinize me for some moments—gave me to understand that she would be either the hellion or the angel of that group. When I told her that I was glad she was going to be in my class, she blushed and said, "I'm glad, too."

She could have been quite a formidable hellion if she'd chosen that path, but before she even attended our first session Hazel was on board with "Paper, Clay, Wood, and Cloth." She was a child who, for whatever reasons, had grown impatient with childhood and who I think was desperate for activities that would challenge and engage her.

It is as hard now as it was then for me to distinguish between what Hazel told me about herself—which wasn't much, really, she wasn't chatty—and what I surmised about her from watching how she behaved. I sometimes felt guilty because my attention was constantly drawn toward Hazel who (without awareness or effort) was an intense presence among the other kids.

What she had, at a ridiculously high level, was focus, and that resource wasn't necessarily to her advantage. She had poor social skills, didn't make friends, seemed to have no athletic ability, paid little attention to her appearance, and could barely tolerate her classmates' childish ways.

I mostly had to give up on assigning her to work with any of the other campers on our projects. To give her credit, she did not try to alienate her co-campers—mostly she just ignored them—and if they became angry with her, she didn't quarrel with them, she just walked away, but she always seemed a little surprised that she'd upset any of them.

For me observing her was a pleasure because in many ways she was absolutely transparent. I was moved by the way she was attracted almost physically to most of the materials we used for our projects—she loved handling the pieces of cedar and pine we used for making small boxes; the bits of cloth we used for making placemats and doll quilts amused her; she liked arranging mosaics out of the beads we used for making necklaces and bracelets; she even made exotic weavings with the strings of colored plastic we used for making lanyards.

Mostly because of Hazel—and because Rock Point had a pond and two small but lively creeks—I introduced a unit on ponds and streams so that we could see and talk about turtles, tadpoles, frogs, salamanders, and birds. To watch that girl lying flat out on the wet grass, conversing earnestly with a turtle, was to understand something profound about both childhood and the world we lose when we become adults.

Those eight students of my morning session became my beloved ones, though I believe that the afternoon class was just as intense and funny and that my success-to-failure rate as a teacher was pretty much the same with both groups. I believe it was because the morning students came to me not exactly straight from bed but when the day was fresh for them and when their dream-life still lingered in their minds.

There was also a slowly evolving change that I witnessed with the morning kids—the group slowly coalescing around Hazel and Hazel unconsciously accepting their begrudging approval. Initially an outcast, that lonely girl—before my eyes—became an unusual version of a leader.

I have to be quick to say that I doubt that Hazel thought of herself as lonely or an outcast or a leader of any kind. As I've said, her first quality as a person was that she possessed focus, though I now realize a therapist might have diagnosed her as unbalanced, a child who needed coaching in social behavior.

If in the first week of our session another child saw Hazel standing still as a stone to watch a blacksnake shed its skin, that child very likely would have laughed at her and summoned other kids to come and look at the weirdo. In the next-to-last week, that same child might slip quietly up beside Hazel and watch the blacksnake with her.

Yes, it's likely I noticed that evolution because Hazel was my favorite—there's no denying that—and I feel neither shame nor guilt for having observed her more carefully than I did the others. I didn't treat her as a favorite, and if I had, Hazel would very likely have lost respect for me.

My point is that she was a constant, and her eight classmates were the ones who changed their attitudes toward her. That dynamic, of the community moving toward harmony, was immensely rewarding for me as both participant and witness.

In the fourth week of the session, in the second week of July, by eleven o'clock the day had become so hot that I opened the classroom door in hopes that a breeze from across the meadow would cool our room down enough that our last hour of the session wouldn't be so sweaty and miserable. I had barely turned back to the children, and the table where we were making origami owls, frogs, and flowers, when two small black forms flew into the room.

Because they were about the size of badminton shuttlecocks, at first I thought they were bats, but almost immediately I saw that they were not darting erratically as bats do but were swooping in arcs over our heads. Only a second or two later I realized they were barn swallows—of the sort that every evening flew over the meadow catching mosquitos and other insects.

The children were shrieking and covering their heads, and Hershel LeTourneau, the biggest boy in the class, had even scooted down out of his chair and seemed to be cowering under the table. I felt the panic of the children but maybe because I was the teacher and the grown-up in the room, I sat still and in that stillness sensed a wave of serenity come over me.

The other person in the room who sat unmoving and who remained in her chair, her head lifted to watch the swallows above our heads, was of course Hazel, and when her eyes met mine I felt—I know this is strange!—so joyful that the girl might have been an angel smiling me at me. I'm certain these were not the words that she meant to convey to me—and probably she was thinking nothing she wanted to share with me, but what I thought in that moment as Hazel and I were perceiving those birds was *like they're little souls frantic to find the bodies from which they've fallen.*

I know that I must have smiled for just that moment, but in Hazel's face I saw—or imagined I saw—her understanding that the swallows were much more terrified than her classmates. They flew toward the windows and scrabbled against the glass, then flew back up into the ceiling space, but in a few seconds they swept down again and fluttered horizontally along the shelf below the glass, wild in their entrapment.

At the same time Hazel and I stood up and turned toward the windows and the birds. I wasn't especially surprised that Hazel and I acted so similarly, as if we'd discussed a plan and had risen together, though I had no notion of what I was going to do beyond moving toward the small black birds.

Swallows swooping in graceful arcs over a meadow or zooming a foot above the grass at twilight are mesmerizing to watch, but they are not likeable creatures—they build nests underneath the eaves of porches; they splatter their poop on porch-floors and railings; and when their babies hatch, they dive-bomb anyone who comes close to their nests. Their sharp beaks and wing-tips and their forked tail-feathers make them look like tiny fighter jets, which is how they behave when they're riled up.

As a grown-up who often returns to Rock Point for spiritual sustenance, I've come to know swallows very well, but at the time those two swept into my classroom, pity for them welled up in me—and probably in my nine-year-old student Hazel as well. Though I believe that I'm a good person and generally an honest and compassionate one, I'm not someone who's ever acted with notable courage or intelligence, and so I'm proud of what Hazel and I managed to do that morning.

That there were the two of us makes all the difference—and really at nine and sixteen years old, I could claim that we were both children. Nowadays I believe everything in that classroom— the birds, the bright day, the shrieking children, the desks, the windows, the vault of space overhead, even the baked-wood fragrance of the room—enchanted Hazel and me so that we were ageless in those moments.

She on one side of the window wall, I on the other, each of us managed with our hands to guide a single bird down into the corner between the glass wall and the shelf that served as a ledge. "Just be really gentle," I murmured, more to myself than to Hazel, "and you can cup them between your two hands."

She caught hers a few moments before I caught mine. Once

we had their wings pinned against their sides, they submitted calmly, with their swiveling heads extending out of the space between our forefingers and thumbs.

When we looked at each other, I smiled because that is how I am, and Hazel merely directly looked at me because that was how she was, but the intensity of her look informed me that her heart was thrumming away in her chest the same as mine was in mine. We both turned to carry the birds to show the children, and as we circled in opposite directions around the tables, they ooohed and aaahed appreciatively and wanted to put their faces right up to within an inch of the birds' beaks and eyes.

Those minutes of showing my campers the swallow in my cupped hands—and I swear I could feel the high-pitched rattle of its heart—foretold my future. I would teach children about the age of these campers, and I would try find opportunities for them to witness the extraordinary events that sometimes happen in ordinary settings.

I walked outside with Hazel close behind me. We walked a little way out into the meadow, which was stunningly green underneath the plain blue sky.

Then we turned to each other. "On three," I murmured, and she nodded.

I sounded the *one* and the *two* very softly, but I shouted the *three*, and we flung our hands and the birds upward. They knew what to do and zoomed up and out away from us, and we knew what to do, too, though I'm certain neither of us had done it before.

We danced a quick-spinning little jig out there on the grass and then stopped and laughed. If on my deathbed I'm granted the memory of a single human face, I'll ask that it be Hazel's, flushed and breathless, just before she and I turned to go back to our classroom.

Acknowledgments

"Golden Gloves," "Little Double Barrel," and "None" appeared in *The Georgia Review.*

"The Arrival of John Robert" appeared in *Harvard Review Online.*

"Ms. Hicks in Hell" appeared in *Numéro Cinq.*

"Prone" and "Swallows" appeared in *Shenandoah.*

"Excruciation" appeared in *The Southern Review.*

RECENT AND SELECTED BOOKS
FROM TUPELO PRESS

Silver Road: Essays, Maps & Calligraphies (hybrid memoir),
Kazim Ali

A Certain Roughness in Their Syntax (poems), Jorge Aulicino,
translated by Judith Filc

Flight (poems), Chaun Ballard

Another English: Anglophone Poems from Around the World
(anthology), edited by Catherine Barnett and Tiphanie Yanique

Everything Broken Up Dances (poems), James Byrne

The Book of LIFE (poems), Joseph Campana

Fire Season (poems), Patrick Coleman

New Cathay: Contemporary Chinese Poetry (anthology),
edited by Ming Di

Calazaza's Delicious Dereliction (poems), Suzanne Dracius,
translated by Nancy Naomi Carlson

Gossip and Metaphysics: Russian Modernist Poetry and Prose
(anthology), edited by Katie Farris, Ilya Kaminsky, and
Valzhyna Mort

Xeixa: Fourteen Catalan Poets (anthology),
edited by Marlon Fick and Francisca Esteve

The Posthumous Affair (novel), James Friel

Native Voices: Indigenous American Poetry, Craft and Conversation,
edited by CMarie Fuhrman and Dean Rader

Leprosarium (poems), Lise Goett

Darktown Follies (poems), Amaud Jamaul Johnson

Dancing in Odessa (poems), Ilya Kaminsky

A God in the House: Poets Talk About Faith (interviews),
edited by Ilya Kaminsky and Katherine Towler

Third Voice (poems), Ruth Ellen Kocher

At the Gate of All Wonder (novel), Kevin McIlvoy

Boat (poems), Christopher Merrill

The Cowherd's Son (poems), Rajiv Mohabir

Marvels of the Invisible (poems), Jenny Molberg

Canto General: Song of the Americas (poems), Pablo Neruda,
translated by Mariela Griffor and Jeffrey Levine

Ex-Voto (poems), Adélia Prado, translated by
Ellen Doré Watson

Intimate: An American Family Photo Album (hybrid memoir),
Paisley Rekdal

Thrill-Bent (novel), Jan Richman

Dirt Eaters (poems), Eliza Rotterman

Good Bones (poems), Maggie Smith

What Could Be Saved (novellas and stories), Gregory Spatz

The Perfect Life (essays), Peter Stitt

Kill Class (poems), Nomi Stone

Swallowing the Sea (essays), Lee Upton

feast gently (poems), G. C. Waldrep

Republic of Mercy (poems), Sharon Wang

Legends of the Slow Explosion (essays), Baron Wormser

See our complete list at www.tupelopress.org

DAVID HUDDLE is the author of seven poetry collections, six short story collections, five novels, a novella, and a collection of essays titled *The Writing Habit*. He won the 2012 Library of Virginia Award for Fiction for *Nothing Can Make Me Do This* and the 2013 Pen New England Award for Poetry for *Blacksnake at the Family Reunion*. Originally from Ivanhoe, Virginia, Huddle has lived in Vermont for nearly fifty years.